"What man doesn't want a beautiful woman?"

Tessa scoffed, tempted to pick up her paper plate and chuck it at him. "I'd rather not join the long list of Josh Donnelly's former girlfriends. I prefer being on the more exclusive 'just friends' list."

"You're at the top of that one. But what's wrong with wanting to be alone with you? After all, it's Monday." They spent every Monday reviewing movie clips in her theater.

She readied the video and sat beside him in the dark theater. Each time she found herself leaning into him, she sat up straight. What was wrong with her?

She attributed the uptick in her heart rate to the heartwarming rom-com preview they'd just watched. After all, this was her best friend, love-'em-and-leave-'em Josh. No one she could ever take seriously.

But even in the darkness, she could see the corner of his mouth turn up in what she called his "killer smile." The smile she'd been immune to.

Till now.

Jean C. Gordon's writing is a natural extension of her love of reading. From that day in first grade when she realized *t-h-e* was the word *the*, she's been reading everything she can put her hands on. Jean and her college-sweetheart husband share a 175-year-old farmhouse in upstate New York with their daughter and her family. Their son lives nearby. Contact Jean at Facebook.com/jeancgordon.author or PO Box 113, Selkirk, NY 12158.

Books by Jean C. Gordon

Love Inspired

The Donnelly Brothers

Winning the Teacher's Heart
Holiday Homecoming
The Bachelor's Sweetheart

Small-Town Sweethearts
Small-Town Dad
Small-Town Mom
Small-Town Midwife

The Bachelor's Sweetheart

Jean C. Gordon

HARLEQUIN® LOVE INSPIRED®

Recycling programs
for this product may
not exist in your area.

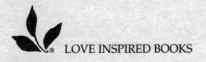 LOVE INSPIRED BOOKS

ISBN-13: 978-0-373-71972-3

The Bachelor's Sweetheart

Copyright © 2016 by Jean Chelikowsky Gordon

www.Harlequin.com

Printed in U.S.A.

In Him we have redemption through His blood,
the forgiveness of sins, in accordance
with the riches of God's grace.
—*Ephesians* 1:7

In memory of my "baby" brother Jim, with thanks to Bonnie Jean, my favorite Drug Court Coordinator and former alcohol counselor, and the guys at the Coeymans Volunteer Fire Department open house who patiently answered all of my questions.

Chapter One

The heat was unbearable, worse than anything Josh Donnelly had ever experienced, even during his National Guard tour of Afghanistan. A rivulet of sweat ran down his back. He wanted to pull at his collar so he could breathe, cool off his back. But people would see him.

"The ring," the guest minister prompted him.

Josh felt like he was aiding and abetting the enemy as he dug in the pocket of his tuxedo jacket. All through high school, after their older brother, Jared, had left Paradox Lake, he'd protected their younger brother, Connor, from their father and the fallout of his being the town drunk. He should be protecting him now from making a potentially huge mistake. Josh handed the wedding band to Connor. Not that his baby brother's soon-to-be wife wasn't a good person. Nor did he doubt that Connor and Natalie Delacroix loved each other— for now.

But the Donnelly men weren't cut out for marriage. That was what he and Jared had always said. They'd agreed they had too much of their father in them to let any woman get close enough to love them. They couldn't risk ultimately hurting someone the way Dad had hurt Mom. That is, they had agreed until last summer when Jared had married Becca Morgan. Now Connor had fallen victim.

Pain squeezed Josh's chest as he caught the loving look on Connor's face when he slipped the ring onto Natalie's finger. *Don't do it.* Josh glanced around to make sure he hadn't said that out loud. He was good. No one was staring at him. No one except his bud Tessa Hamilton, who was sitting halfway back in the church, her bulletin covering her mouth, eyes sparkling. She was laughing at him.

Tessa knew how he felt about marriage and didn't hold it against him—one of the many reasons they got along so well. But that didn't mean he was going to let her get away with laughing at his discomfort. Josh smiled to himself. He had the perfect revenge. He'd ask her to dance at the wedding reception. Tessa didn't dance. She said her dancing wasn't for public consumption.

"I now pronounce you husband and wife," the minister declared. "You can kiss your bride."

Connor pressed his lips to Natalie's. Then they turned and faced the guests hand in hand.

"I present Mr. and Mrs. Connor Donnelly," the minister said.

The guests stood and applauded. Josh's gaze went to his mother, who was standing next to his grandmother and stepgrandfather, Harry, in the front pew. Harry smiled down at Grandma with almost the same expression Connor had had when he'd slipped the ring on Natalie's finger. Josh glanced across the aisle to Natalie's parents. Terry and John Delacroix stood hand in hand much like Connor and Natalie. Connor *was* different than him and Jared, more like their mother—although Jared appeared to have become the poster boy for marital bliss. And Connor was a minister, the pastor here at Hazardtown Community Church. Maybe he and Natalie would make it work.

The organist began the recessional and the applause stopped. As Connor and Natalie started up the aisle, Josh stepped front and center and offered his arm to Claire Delacroix, Natalie's sister and maid of honor. Jared fell into step behind them with Natalie's oldest sister, Andrea Bissette, and the rest of the wedding party.

Josh bit the side of his mouth to keep from laughing as he passed Tessa and she glanced from him to Claire with a raised eyebrow. Tessa had been trying to fix him up with Natalie's sister since Connor and Natalie became engaged last Christmas. And Connor had been warning him off as if he wasn't good enough for Connor's future sister-in-law. At one point, Josh had considered asking Claire out just to irritate Connor but had thought better of it. Why jeopardize the brotherly bond for a woman he'd only move on from in a month or two? Not that there were many available women left in Paradox Lake for him to move on to. Even more reason for him to finish his engineering technology degree and blow this burg.

The wedding party lined up with his mother and Natalie's parents outside at the bottom of the church steps to greet the guests. Their grandparents were the first in line.

"You're next," his grandmother said when she reached him in the line. Her husband chuckled. A chill ran down Josh's spine, remembering Gram saying something on that order about Jared before he succumbed to Becca's charms.

"Josh and Claire do make a cute couple," Claire's grandmother added, kissing Claire on her cheek.

"Oh, Marie, I thought I'd told you he's seeing Tessa Hamilton, Betty's granddaughter."

Marie Delacroix nodded with a sympathetic look at Claire. Josh smiled at the lovingly tolerant look Claire returned. Being in their early thirties, he and Claire were fortunate to still have their grandmothers.

"Gram," he said, "Tessa and I are friends. That's all."

"Famous last words. Jared and Becca and Connor and Natalie were friends first, too."

Josh looked over his grandmother's head at her husband, who chuckled again. "Edna, we're holding up the line."

Gram gave Harry "the look," the one that Josh recognized as a silent "you're pushing it." But she continued down the line, giving Jared a hug and telling him how handsome he looked. Friends and family filed by behind his grandmother, shaking his hand and exchanging small talk.

"Natalie, I'm so happy for you and Connor."

Josh's ears perked up at the sound of Tessa's voice. A smile spread across his face as he thought about his plans for the reception.

"Josh, this is my uncle," Claire said, breaking his private gloat.

"Nice to meet you," he said, shaking the man's hand.

Tessa stepped up next. "Claire, you look beautiful. I love the bridesmaid dresses."

Some guy Josh didn't recognize stood close behind Tessa, as if he was with her.

"I know." Claire dropped her voice. "I was thinking I wouldn't be embarrassed to wear the dress again in public."

Josh narrowed his eyes, thinking back to the ceremony. *A date?* He didn't remember seeing anyone sitting close enough to Tessa in the pew to suggest they were with her. Tessa stepped in front of him, and the man bent and gave Claire a hug.

"Hi," Tessa said. "I see you didn't expire up there. For a minute it looked touch and go."

He ran his gaze across her face, masking the irritation her comment ignited. He'd had things in hand up at the altar, totally in control. His mood softened. Tessa looked different. Her rich chestnut hair was down, softly framing her face. And her eyes…he couldn't put his finger on it. They were different, more defined. He dropped his focus to her lips and took in the pink sheen along with the creamy tan of her flawless skin. *Makeup.* He stared at her. *Tessa was wearing makeup.*

"What?" she said. "Are you so traumatized you can't talk?"

"You look nice."

She blinked and drew her head back.

Smooth, Donnelly. Way to give a compliment. But he was used to seeing Tessa on a buddy level.

"As in not how I usually look?" Tessa tilted her head and drilled her gaze into his.

"Yeah." It slipped out as if his mouth had no connection to his brain. Time to bring out the reinforcements. Josh drew his mouth into the slow half smile that always worked on women. "Unbelievably, you look even more beautiful than usual."

Tessa rolled her eyes. *She rolled her eyes.* Not dating for the past few months had put him more out of practice than he'd thought. The Smile always used to work.

"Catch you later at the reception." He nodded toward

the people lined up behind her and squelched the urge to glare at the man in front of him.

"This is my cousin Pierre, from Montreal," Claire said.

Josh sized up the competition as they shook hands. "Nice to meet you."

"Ravi de vous rencontrer également," Pierre said.

Josh's gaze pierced the back of Pierre's head as he moved on. Was the guy showing off, or didn't he speak English? Josh shook his head. He didn't know what had gotten into him. There was no competition. Josh liked Tessa too much to let their relationship become anything more than a friendship.

Tessa waited for her grandmother on the sidewalk in front of the church, a small distance from the group of friends and relatives gathering there. She didn't quite feel part of them, even though she'd been in the area and belonged to Hazardtown Community Church for several years. She'd caught the glare Josh had given Claire's cousin. Pierre must have gone along with her suggestion he speak to Josh in French. She'd told him that Josh was working on his French for a possible promotion to a position in Quebec. It was essentially true. Josh's employer, GreenSpaces, had an office in Quebec, and Josh's ambition was to fast-track himself up the corporate ladder by whatever route was available. And his French *was* awful.

If she didn't know better, she'd think Josh was jealous. Tessa studied the rugged lines of his profile and gave in to the momentary pleasure of having a man as attractive as Josh show an interest in her. But he'd better not be going in that direction. She had it from his own mouth that his love-'em-and-leave-'em reputation was dead-on, and her record in romance was dismal. Tessa followed the line of people from Josh to her grand-mother and lifted her hand to let Grandma know where she was in the growing crowd on the sidewalk. No, she wasn't going to let Josh think about the possibility of them being anything but friends. Not now when she was going to need his friendship and help more than ever.

Her grandmother joined her. "Edna said the wedding party is going down to the lake for some photos, but we guests can go to the church hall for hors d'oeuvres while we wait."

Tessa listened to the birds chirping as they walked around to the hall door at the back of the church building. The early-afternoon sun promised the day would meet the record spring temperature the TV meteorologist had forecast.

"Connor and Natalie certainly have a gorgeous day for their wedding, considering it's only late April and we had piles of snow left a week and a half ago. I'm sure their photos at the lake will be beautiful," Tessa said.

"The wedding would have been lovely, even if we'd had a blizzard," her grandmother said. "Natalie and Connor are perfect for each other, although it took them long enough to figure that out."

Tessa stifled a laugh. Her grandmother, along with many of the other parishioners at Hazardtown Community Church, had started working on marrying off Connor almost as soon as he'd accepted his calling there.

"Connor and Jared have come so far, despite the stigma of their father," her grandmother said. "They do their mother proud."

Tessa didn't miss that her grandmother had left out Josh, who was as successful as his brothers, if not as out-wardly upstanding and charitable. Jared had selflessly invested a great deal of his racing winnings in bringing his motocross school to Paradox Lake to help the local economy and employment situation. Connor was their beloved pastor, at least now, after getting off to a rocky start with some of his congregation. Josh was a good man, too. Sympathy welled in her. He didn't show enough people the real Josh she knew.

She wished Grandma could see that. Tessa knew her grandmother didn't really approve of their friendship. But if Josh would agree to her plan, she was sure Grandma would change her mind about him. Maybe because they were just friends and that's all they'd ever be, Tessa was confident Josh was the one time her man intuition was correct. Taking and releasing a breath, she opened the hall door for her grandmother.

"Oh, good," her grandmother said, looking at the place cards at one of the round tables next to the long wedding party table near the door. "I'm sitting with Edna and Harry and Marie. I didn't know if I would be, them being the grandparents."

Tessa wasn't surprised. Natalie knew how close the three women were, and not many of their generation were left in the church. "You go ahead and get something to eat, if you want. I'll look for my seat." A pang of loneliness struck Tessa as her grandmother joined her friends at the hot hors d'oeuvres station. Tessa walked around the hall, looking for her place card, and found it at a table with other members of the church singles group. Without the bride and groom, and Josh and Claire in the wedding party, the group barely filled the eight-person table.

After grabbing a cup of tea and some veggies to munch on, Tessa returned to the table to find Lexi Zarinski, one of Josh's many former girlfriends, and a couple of acquaintances seated at the table. The table makeup reminded Tessa that almost all of her friends were married now. Hitting thirty was apparently the clock striking midnight on the single life. She chatted with the group through dinner, intermittently glancing across the room to check on her grandmother, who appeared to be thoroughly enjoying her friends, and on Josh. She needed to catch him and find out when they could talk, preferably tonight.

When they'd finished eating, the DJ put on "Yours Forever." Connor rose, took Natalie's hand and led her to the dance floor in the middle of the room. "Natalie is so beautiful," Lexi gushed, going into a monologue of every detail of the bride's gown and why it was perfect for her.

"And don't Claire and Josh make a great couple?" Tessa interrupted Lexi's soliloquy as Josh led Claire to the dance floor when the DJ invited the wedding party to join the bride and groom. If Josh ever got his act together concerning women, he and Claire were perfect for each other.

Lexi pinched her lips together, and Tessa regretted her casual observation. Apparently, Lexi still had feelings for Josh. One of the guys at the table asked Lexi to dance, ending the awkward moment. Tessa tapped her foot to the music under the table, totally out of time, she was sure, but no one would notice.

"And now, by request," the DJ said several songs later, "The Chicken Dance."

"I didn't think anyone did the Chicken Dance at weddings anymore," Lexi said.

"I haven't heard it since I was a kid," someone else remarked.

Tessa surveyed the room, trying to figure out who

might have made the request. She saw Josh making a straight line for her table. Lexi did, too. She sat up and fluffed her hair.

"Hey," Josh greeted everyone around the table.

When he got to Lexi, she smiled and started to push her chair back, obviously assuming he'd come over to ask her to dance. She and Tessa were the only two women at the table right then.

"Tessa, it's our dance," he said with a grin.

She shook her head with sympathy for Lexi. Josh might be able to tear out all the roots of a relationship when he called it quits, but didn't he realize most other people couldn't?

"Come on," he urged. His dark-lashed, deep blue eyes challenged her.

He was up to something. He knew she didn't dance.

Tessa stood and offered Josh her hand. "You're on."

Whatever Josh was up to, she was game. If making a fool of herself in front of everyone she knew in the area by dancing the silly Chicken Dance would humor Josh and make him more agreeable to what she needed to ask of him, she'd do it. *For Grandma.*

Josh eyed Tessa. This was too easy. She was giving in with no protest. What fun was that? He led her toward the center of the room. "We don't have to…" He gestured at the people flapping their elbows on the dance floor.

The corner of her mouth quirked up.

"Okay, so I asked you to dance because you laughed at me up at the altar." He rubbed the back of his neck as the childishness of his words registered. When had he regressed to being ten years old?

"So, you don't really want to join them?" She mimicked his gesture to the people hopping around in front of them.

"You have to ask?" Josh toed for a foothold on some semblance of his dignity.

"No, not about that, but I have something else I want to ask you about. Let's take a walk outside where we don't have to talk over the music and everyone else."

"As long as it's not about Claire's cousin." Josh scuffed the toe of his shoe against the tile floor. His wedding-aversion mouth-to-brain disconnect had kicked in again.

"What do you mean?" She faced him, hands on hips. After a second, her eyes brightened. "Oh, Claire told you."

His mind flipped back through his dinner conversation with Claire and came up blank.

Tessa laughed. "I told Pierre to speak French, said you were working on improving your French for a possible job transfer to Quebec."

"Oh, that." He waved her off.

"Yeah, what did you think?"

"I just wasn't following. All this—"

"Wedding stuff," she finished for him as they crossed the hall to the door.

"Enough said." Tessa so got him. He couldn't ask for a better friend. Josh gave her a side glance. Or one easier on the eyes. "What do you need to talk about?"

"I have a business proposition."

He held the door open for Tessa, and they strolled outside to a picnic table. It had to be about the movie theater in Schroon Lake she'd inherited from her grandfather Hamilton a few years ago and reopened as the Majestic. Josh knew the business was touch and go in terms of providing a living for her and her grandmother. If he were her, he'd have sold the theater and gone back to the civil engineering career she'd had before she'd moved in with her grandmother to run the theater. But he wasn't her. Josh swung his leg over the wooden bench.

"You still with me?" Tessa asked, breaking the silence of his thoughts.

"I'm listening."

"I've come up with financing for my plan to renovate the Majestic to do dinner theater in addition to movies during the summer tourist season."

Josh leaned forward on his forearms. "The credit union approved a mortgage on the theater building?" He was surprised. All of the banks in the area had already turned Tessa down.

She shifted on the bench. "No, the loan officer suggested a mortgage on Grandma's house."

That made sense to Josh since the well-kept Victorian would be much easier to sell than the old theater building.

"I couldn't ask Grandma to do that."

"But you said you got financing."

Tessa studied her nails, which were a soft shade of pink. With sparkles. He'd never seen her nails polished before. She'd gone all out for this wedding. Why? He took in the complete package from the soft wisps of hair framing her face to the delicate red-and-silver hearts dangling from her ears to her sparkling fingers. Whatever, she should do it more often.

"From Jared."

Josh straightened. "You went to my brother." *Good old Jared; always ready to step in and save the day.* Old wounds of sibling rivalry ripped open.

"No, he came to me. I thought you knew. He said you

told him about my plans and the trouble I was having with the financing."

"Yeah, I did." But not in a good way. He'd been feeling Jared out for a way to discourage Tessa from what he saw as a potential financial disaster.

"Anyway, he called the other night, and we got together yesterday. You know how he is about supporting local businesses. I think he'd hate to see the Majestic go under almost as much as I would. He suggested a couple of things that could make the plan more successful."

Josh ground his teeth then relaxed his jaw. *Admit it, Donnelly. You're jealous. Tessa is your friend, and you want to be the one to rescue her from her financial plight, although with a more lucrative plan than saving her struggling theater business.* Tessa had too much potential to stagnate in Schroon Lake.

"Hey," Tessa said. "Lose the face. I would have called you last night, but you had the wedding rehearsal and all."

"Sorry, I've had a lot on my mind."

"Like how to talk Connor out of marrying the love of his life."

Josh grinned. "That and other things. Tell me what Jared suggested."

"He can't give me as much of a loan as I was asking the banks for." Tessa gave a number that was about twenty thousand short of what Josh knew she needed.

"We went over those numbers," he said. "I can't see how you can get the job done for any less."

Tessa gestured palms up, fingers splayed. "That's where you come in, why I needed to talk with you."

He read the excitement on her face, and his stomach churned. He had some money invested from the couple of lakeside cabins he bought cheap, remodeled and flipped for a profit. But not money to lend, like his brother, the ex-international motocross champion. His stash was to finance his move away from Paradox Lake when the right promotion came along. He needed to have a good long talk with his brother about putting him in this situation.

"Tessa, I don't have that kind of money."

"I know that. I wouldn't think of asking you for money."

But she'd ask Jared. He placed his hands palms down on the table. Just give him another five years and he'd be as successful in his own right as his older brother was.

"What I need from you is your brawn and brains."

He burst out laughing. "Brawn and brains."

"That doesn't appeal to your masculinity?" She batted her eyelashes at him.

She was going to have him rolling on the ground soon.

Her expression grew serious. "Here's my proposal. First, since I'd only be doing the dinner theater a couple of nights a week, Jared suggested I have the dinners catered by that new restaurant that's opening on State Route 74, rather than add full kitchen facilities. I'd only need a refrigerator-freezer and an industrial warming oven."

"That makes sense." So much sense, he wished he'd thought of it, except he hadn't been encouraging Tessa in her project.

"Second, in exchange for you helping me make the other necessary alterations to the theater building, you could live rent-free in the apartment over the garage adjacent to the theater and Grandma's house. Then, once I open, I'll give you a twenty percent cut of the Majestic's profits until you've been fully paid for your time." She tilted her head so the rays of the setting sun reflected the expectant look in her soft brown eyes. "What do you say?"

A great plan except that he didn't expect there to be any profits to pay him from.

In response to his hesitation, she prompted, "The sale closing on the cabin is still next week so you have to be out, right? And you don't have anyplace to live."

No place but with one of his brothers or back with Gram and Harry again as he'd done when he first returned to Paradox Lake to take the job at GreenSpaces.

"Or did you find a rental?" she asked.

"The closing is next Thursday, and I haven't found anything long-term, only a couple of places that are available to rent until late June when the summer people start arriving."

"Then you'll do it? I'll have the attorney who settled Grandpa's estate draw up a contract next week."

Since he didn't have much confidence in the project paying out, as a friend, he should say no. But as a friend, he knew how much it meant to Tessa to stay in Schroon Lake and run the Majestic, even though he didn't fully understand why. She could do so much more with her life.

"Sure. It's a deal."

Chapter Two

Tessa hugged herself for warmth as she walked the short distance from the Majestic to her grandmother's house. The unusually warm spring day had turned frosty with nightfall, and the light coat she'd worn to the wedding wasn't enough to ward off the chill of the air or her thoughts.

After dropping her grandmother off at the house, she'd gone over to the movie house, figuring her part-time college student employee, Myles, would be closing up about then. She should have waited until he checked in with her in the morning as she'd asked him to do. The Saturday night—generally her biggest night—receipts were dismal. And she couldn't attribute it all to the large number of people attending Connor and Natalie's wedding. As her grandmother's house came in view, the moon and streetlight spotlighted the shutter on the second-floor window the winter winds had knocked askew. The theater building wasn't alone in needing work, although all the house needed was some cosmetic touches and basic upkeep. Maybe she could extend Josh's contract to cover whatever she couldn't do on the house herself.

Tessa trudged up the steps of the house she and her grandmother shared and stepped into the living room. She locked the front door behind her. Before she'd moved in with her, her grandmother had never locked her doors when she was home. She'd finally convinced her they should at least lock up at night. "Grandma, I'm back."

"I'm in the kitchen," she answered.

Tessa slipped off her coat and reached in the pocket for her phone when her text alert chimed. She frowned at the name.

"Your uncle Bob?" Grandma stood in the doorway drying her hands on a dish towel.

"Yes." Tessa read the text.

I need you to work on your grandmother. Maybe she'll listen to you. We're going to lose the introductory price on the condos if she doesn't agree soon.

"I just got off the phone with him before you came in." Her grandmother sighed. "I guess I have to make a final decision. Maybe I should take the train down to Albany and let Bob show me around the community he and Kathy are moving to. But I can't imagine living someplace where everyone is over fifty-five. I think being around you kids helps keep me young."

Tessa smiled at her grandmother's last comment as she hung her coat in the closet. "I thought you had decided you didn't want to leave Schroon Lake and all of your friends."

"Come on into the kitchen." Her grandmother avoided her question, waving the dish towel toward the doorway. "We need to talk."

Tessa tensed.

"I put some water on for chamomile tea. I shouldn't have had that second cup of coffee at the reception. It's past my usual bedtime, and I'm not at all sleepy."

Tessa followed her into the kitchen. She could use something calming, too. An old longing awoke. Even after five years, the craving for alcohol was there deep inside her. She breathed in. *Lord.* And out. *Help me.* "Tea would be great."

Grandma's old metal teakettle began to whistle when they walked into the kitchen.

"Grab a couple of mugs, spoons and the tea tin." Her grandmother bustled over to the stove, turned off the gas and lifted the kettle from the burner. "And the hot plate from the dish drainer. Since it's just the two of us, I'm not going to bother with a teapot."

Tessa had the mugs, tea and hot plate on the table when her grandmother brought the kettle over. She put a tea bag in each mug, and her grandmother filled them with boiling water.

They sat next to each other at the small round table.

"You're the only one in the family who drinks tea plain, like me," her grandmother said.

Tessa stirred her drink, watching the tea bag swirl around. She pressed it against the side of the mug and placed the tea bag and spoon on the table. "But we didn't come in here to talk about tea or sugar. What happened to your decision to stay in Schroon Lake?"

Her grandmother dropped her gaze to the mug of tea sitting in front of her. "I found out how little you have left of the money your grandfather gave you to make a go of the Majestic."

Tessa started. Grandma wasn't a person to go snooping around in other people's business. "How?"

"I went paperless with my bank statements and was

having trouble printing them out from the bank's website. I stopped in at the bank to see if someone could show me what I was doing wrong. Along with my other accounts, the bank officer gave me the statement from the joint checking account your grandfather set up for you when he was sick. He must have put me on the account, too."

"I wasn't hiding it from you." Tessa couldn't keep the defensive note out of her voice. The days when she purposely hid her actions were over. "I didn't want to worry you while I figured out what we were going to do."

Her grandmother reached over and squeezed her hand. "Honey, you don't have to struggle for me. Your grandfather didn't leave you the theater to tie you to it or me or Schroon Lake. He left it as an option, if you wanted to come and run it while you figured out what you really wanted to do. You didn't seem happy with your engineering job with the State Department of Transportation in Albany."

"I wasn't. But I don't want you to have to leave everything you love because I didn't come through for you."

Grandma and Grandpa had been there for her when her parents hadn't been. They'd opened their home to her for school breaks when she'd been partying her way to disaster her first year at college because she was trying so hard to fit in. They'd given her nonjudgmental guidance to right herself with God and go back to college her second year. They'd stood by her when Blake had broken their engagement because he'd found even her "controlled" drinking a problem, and afterward when she'd fallen into a spiral of binging that had landed her in rehab.

"We loved you. You do for those you love. You don't

owe me anything. And it's not like you'd leave me out on the street, or that I'd have to move away, unless I want to. Who knows, if I go see those condos Bob is hounding me about, I might like them. And Marie Delacroix has mentioned several times that she wouldn't mind having someone share her house with her. It's smaller than this monstrosity and easier to manage."

"But you love this monstrosity, and I have a plan that will let us stay right here." Tessa explained Jared's loan and Josh's agreement to help her with the work.

Her grandmother's eyes narrowed. "You've thought this through, prayed on it? It sounds to me like you'd be taking on a lot. A loan, all that remodeling. How much time will Josh have to help you? Edna says he practically lives in his office at GreenSpaces. Besides, didn't you tell me he wasn't so keen on the dinner theater idea?"

Tessa raised her empty mug to her lips to hide the disappointment she was afraid would show on her face. She swallowed. "That was before Jared suggested a couple of ways to reduce expenses, and I offered Josh free rent on the apartment above the garage."

"Has he seen the apartment?" her grandmother asked, her smile and the twinkle in her eye breaking the tension.

Tessa laughed. "No, I have my work cut out for me tomorrow."

"You are so sweet to want to do this for me."

"It's for me, too. Grandpa had faith in me. I love the Majestic as much as he did."

Her grandmother's smile faded. "As long as you're doing this for yourself and not for him. He wouldn't want that."

Tessa nodded and rose to rinse her mug in the sink.

Grandma was right about her having to live for herself. She'd lived most of her life trying her best to do, be, what her parents wanted. So they'd be proud of her, love her. That certainly hadn't worked out as she'd wanted.

"And to be an interfering old woman, watch that Josh Donnelly. You know his reputation. I would hate to see your heart broken again."

She squirted dish detergent in the mug and turned on the faucet. "I know *all* about Josh Donnelly. You don't have to worry about me seeing him as anything but a buddy."

Midday Wednesday Josh pulled his pickup into the small parking lot beside the attorney's office. When Tessa had called him about setting a time for an appointment to sign their contract, he'd asked her if she could schedule it at lunchtime today, so he wouldn't have to take extra time off work. He'd already scheduled a half day of vacation for this afternoon to talk to his little sister Hope's third grade class for career day. It wasn't that he didn't have vacation time accrued, lots of vacation time. But he was really into the project he was working on directly with the owner of GreenSpaces, Anne Hazard, and he might need some of that time later to help Tessa.

He tossed his shades onto the passenger-side seat and glanced in the rearview mirror, running his hand over his hair. He and Tessa didn't need all the formality she was insisting on. She couldn't think he'd bail on a less-formal agreement. She was his best friend, probably his only real friend, except for his brothers. There were the people he hung out with at work, the singles group at church and the vets at the American Legion in Ticonderoga, but they were more acquaintances. He hadn't connected with any of them like he had with Tessa. As for his high school friends still in the area, they were better avoided.

A motion in the mirror caught his eye. Tessa waved from the sidewalk in front of the law office. He unfolded himself from the truck and strode over, battling the uncertainty that he couldn't seem to shake about the wisdom of this deal.

"Hi," Tessa said, "right on time."

"Would you expect anything less?" He opened the door to the building and motioned her to go in first.

"Not with you and a business deal."

He let the door snap shut behind him. *Ambition was a good quality.* He bristled. *It kept food on the table.*

The attorney met them in the reception area. He was probably anxious to get to his lunch. At the thought of food, Josh's stomach rumbled. He hadn't had lunch, thinking he and Tessa could grab something together quick before he had to be at the school.

"Ms. Hamilton, Mr. Donnelly, come right back to my office. I have the agreement all ready."

Josh and Tessa took the two seats in front of the desk.

"How's that little sister of yours?" the attorney asked.

"She's doing well with Jared and Becca. Fits right in with Becca's two kids." Tessa's attorney was the same one Jared had used to get custody of their orphaned half sister, Hope, last year. "I'm going over to the school to talk to her class about my job for career day when we finish here."

"Let's get going then." The attorney gave each of them a copy of the contract. "Take your time. Read it thoroughly and ask me any questions you have."

Tessa skimmed over the two pages and placed them on the desk in front of her, while Josh read every word.

He went back to the clause about paying him 20 percent of the Majestic profits until his time was paid for at the rate he and Tessa had agreed to verbally.

"What would happen if the profits aren't enough to pay me my percentage and cover Tessa and her grandmother's living expenses?"

Tessa bristled. "Don't worry, Josh. You'll get paid."

He shook his head slowly. Maybe she didn't know him as well as he thought she did. He was ambitious, not callous. "My concern is for you being obligated to pay me money you might not have."

She pressed a fist to her lips and dropped it to her lap. "Then why did you agree to do the work?" The hurt in her eyes spoke her unsaid words. *You don't think I'll succeed.*

Now he'd insulted her. But he did have doubts about the project's viability and didn't want to put Tessa and her grandmother in financial straits again.

"Do you two need a moment to discuss things?" the attorney asked, glancing at the clock.

From what Josh figured Tessa had told the attorney, the man had probably thought this was a ten-minute slam-dunk done deal.

"I want to do the work." Josh looked from the attorney to Tessa. "Can we add a profit threshold where payments to me would kick in? It could be based on the average monthly cost of living for a two-person household in Essex County."

"I could do that," the attorney said. "Let me check that figure. Or do you need to think about it, Ms. Hamilton?" He typed into his computer while he waited for her answer.

"I can come back later, after I'm done at the school," Josh said.

"It's fine," Tessa said in a tone that didn't support her words.

"I've got that figure." The attorney wrote the numbers on a pad and turned it toward them.

"The amount looks reasonable to me," Tessa said.

Josh thought it looked low, compared to what he brought in as a senior drafter at GreenSpaces and what he knew Tessa must have earned as a civil engineer for the state. He pressed his lips together to prevent any of the brain-mouth disconnect he'd suffered with Tessa last Saturday. "Okay, Tessa will be obligated to pay my cut only after the safety-net amount has been reached. And, as it already reads, if I can't finish the work for any reason, she'll owe no royalties and I'll reimburse her fair rental for any time I've been in the apartment."

Tessa hadn't liked that clause, but he had to protect her, both of them, if he received a promotion offer from one of the other GreenSpaces offices.

"Correct," the attorney confirmed. "If you have ten minutes, I can type the change in and print out a new agreement for you to sign, unless you have any other questions or problems."

"No, I'm good, and I don't have to be at the school until one."

"I can stay, too," Tessa said. She pulled out her cell phone and tapped on the screen while the attorney made the changes. The room was quiet, except for the click of the computer keyboard, followed by the whirr of the laser printer on the other side of the room.

"I'll get those." Josh was out of his seat before the attorney could even push his chair away from the computer.

Taking his copy from the top, he handed the other one to Tessa, sat and reread the revised clause. When he'd finished, Tessa already had a pen in hand, ready to sign.

"Looks okay to me," he said, picking up the other pen the attorney had laid out on the desk.

"Hold off on signing until I get someone to witness your signatures." The attorney left them alone in the office.

"You are all right with my change?" Josh asked, breaking the silence.

"I guess I have to be. No one else will do the work as cheaply as you will."

"You got other bids?"

"No," she shot back. "But I thought you had more faith in me."

"I have plenty of faith in you. It's the tourist trade I'm not so sure of."

The attorney returned with Josh's former girlfriend. "This is Lexi Zarinski. She's filling in for the next few days while our receptionist is on vacation."

"I know Josh and Tessa from church. Hi."

"Hi." Josh and Tessa signed and dated the agreement. The attorney took both agreements and placed the second sheet with the witness signature line on top.

Lexi signed them both with a flourish. "I'm taking my lunch break now. Do you guys want to join me at the diner?" Although Lexi had included Tessa in her invitation, her gaze rested on Josh. He rearranged the pages of the agreement on the desk in front of him.

"Sorry, I've got to get over to the school. I'm telling Hope's class about my job for career day."

"And I told Grandma I'd go with her to her doctor's appointment in Ticonderoga."

"Okay, maybe another time." Lexi made her exit.

The attorney rose and shook their hands. "Nice seeing both of you again."

"Thanks," Tessa said.

Josh nodded. He looked around for Lexi lurking as they walked across the reception area to the door. "I was going to ask you if you wanted to get some lunch, but I don't have time now."

"I would have taken you up on the offer. Maybe even treated to make up for my outburst about you getting paid." She stopped when they reached the sidewalk and looked up at him. "You know, I could just hug you for what you're doing for Grandma and me."

After the way Tessa's glamorous appearance at the wedding had affected him, he was glad she didn't.

Josh grabbed his laptop from behind the driver's seat before he headed into the building that housed the Schroon Lake Central School, grades kindergarten through twelve, his alma mater. He signed in at the main office with Thelma Woods, who'd been the office manager for as long as he could remember.

"The third grade room is the same as it's always been," Mrs. Woods said.

"Okay, and I'll be taking Hope home after school."

She leafed through a small pile of papers clipped together. "Yes, I have the note from Becca right here. You'll need to sign out before you leave."

"Will do."

"Josh." Hope called to him as he left the office.

He waved at his sister.

A middle-aged woman was leading a group of kids including Hope down the hall past the office. She stopped. "Mr. Donnelly?"

"Josh." He offered his hand.

"I'm Merilee Bradshaw, Hope's teacher. We're on our way back from lunch. You can walk with us."

He stepped in line with Hope.

"Is that your daddy?" the little boy in front of her asked.

"No," Hope huffed. "Like I told everybody, Josh is my brother. I have three big brothers. Jared, who I live with. He talked to our class last year. Mrs. Bradshaw said we had to have different people this year. Connor. He's the pastor at my church and on his honeymoon with Natalie, so he couldn't come today. And Josh."

Josh shook off the pang of hurt that he was apparently Hope's third choice. "Who's your friend?" He nodded at the little boy.

"Owen Maddox, and he's not a friend. He's a boy."

"Can't boys be friends? Tessa is my friend, and she's a girl."

"You're a grown-up, and she's your girlfriend. That's different."

"No, she's just a friend who's a girl."

Hope looked skeptical. *Gram at the wedding, now Hope.* What was so hard for everyone to get about Tessa and him being friends, not a couple?

"Our room is the next one," Hope said.

"I know. It was my third grade room, and Jared and Connor's, too."

Mrs. Bradshaw stood at the classroom doorway, counting heads as the kids filed in. She closed the door behind her last student. "Everyone put your lunch boxes in your cubbies, so we can hear Mr. Donnelly's talk."

Josh waited for his sister and, when she finished, she led him to the middle of the room. "This is my desk, and this is my friend Ava."

"Hi," the little girl at the desk beside Hope's said.

She eyed his laptop. "Are you going to show us racing videos like Hope's other brother did last year? They were really cool."

Yeah. Josh was sure they were. Jared was cool. "No, we're going to design a solar-powered go-cart."

"But you didn't bring any wood or stuff."

"On the computer. You'll see everything we do on the screen up front." Josh had thought the kids would like brainstorming ideas for a go-cart and using the computer-aided design program to draw plans. His talk was hands-on. He planned to let the kids come up and use the program to add their details. And he'd gotten permission from his boss to print out copies of the plans at work for Hope to bring in and hand out to everyone on Friday.

"Oh," Ava said.

"Mr. Donnelly, we're ready."

Despite the lack of enthusiasm from Hope's friend Ava, the talk went as well or better than Josh had hoped. The kids had some great and outlandish ideas. And Josh seemed to have made a friend in Hope's non-friend, Owen. The little boy latched on to him to the point of asking if he wanted to sit next to him at his desk for the second job presentation of the afternoon. With Hope's permission, he did.

"Class, let's thank Ms. Foster and Mr. Donnelly for talking to us today," the teacher said when the other speaker had finished her presentation.

"Thank you, Ms. Foster and Mr. Donnelly," the classed chimed.

A bell rang.

"That means the buses are here," Hope said.

"Everyone get your things together and line up," Mrs. Bradshaw said.

She led the queue of third graders to the main door while Jared and Hope headed to the office to sign out. Owen trailed behind them.

Josh stopped. "Owen, don't you need to get on your bus?"

"No, I wait for my mom in the office. She's a teacher's aide. Can I ask you a question?"

"Sure." Josh hoped he wouldn't regret his hasty agreement.

"You know a lot about go-carts. Have you ever made a Pinewood Derby racer?"

"No, I haven't. I wasn't a Boy Scout. But my nephew made one."

"I want to make one, but Mom doesn't know anything about building things." Owen stared at his feet. "And my dad's at Dannemora. We moved here so it's not so far to drive to visit him."

Josh swallowed the lump in his throat. *The maximum security Clinton Correctional Facility.* Although his father had never been in more than the county jail for a few days, Josh could certainly relate to an absent father.

"With all the stuff you know, we could make a winner."

He squatted to Owen's level. "I can't make any promises, but who's your Scout leader?"

"Mr. Hazard."

"I know Mr. Hazard. I'll talk with him and see what I can do, okay?"

A smile lit Owen's face. "Okay!"

"I'll have to have your mother's permission to help you."

"You can wait with me now and talk to her today."

Josh stood. "No, I want to talk to Mr. Hazard first."

"All right." Owen took a seat in the office, and Josh signed Hope and him out.

"Bye," Owen said as they left. "See you tomorrow, Hope."

"Bye, Owen." Hope's goodbye sounded friendly enough. If it hadn't, he would have had to have a talk with her, which wouldn't be in sync with the fun-brother persona he cultivated. Hope's situation as the new kid last school year hadn't been a lot different from Owen's.

"Can we build something, too?" she asked as he made sure she had the seat belt buckled across her booster seat correctly.

"What do you want to build?" If he didn't watch it, he'd have so many projects going he'd have to take a leave of absence from his real job to do them all.

"A castle in the backyard at my house."

"I'll need to talk with Jared and Becca about that one."

"All right, but I'm sure it will be okay."

Josh wasn't as sure. "I missed lunch. What do you say to an ice cream sundae at the diner while I get a burger and fries?"

"I say yes. Becca and Jared only let us get cones."

Score one for big brother Josh. Since he didn't plan on having any kids of his own, didn't have it in him to be a husband and father, he figured it was his place to spoil Hope and Jared and Becca's family and any kids Connor and Natalie might have.

Hope caught him up on everything third grade while he ate his late lunch.

"Be sure to talk to Jared," Hope said when he walked her into the house.

"Talk to me about what?" Jared asked, walking in behind them.

"Tell him, Josh." Hope scampered off to the other room.

"Hope asked me to build her a castle in your backyard. I assume she means a playhouse castle."

"Better check that. With Hope, you never know. She could mean a full-scale stone-wall moat-surrounded castle."

Josh laughed.

"I don't see a problem. I'll talk with Becca, and you can work the details out with our little sister."

"I have something else I want to talk with you about."

"My loan to Tessa? It's the same as the loans I've made to other local businesses. It has nothing to do with whatever you two have going on."

Jared, too? "Friends. We're friends. And that's not what I wanted to talk with you about. It's her loan, her business. What I want to talk to you about is a little boy in Hope's class, Owen. He sounds like a good candidate for your motocross school program. His mom's a teacher's aide at the school, and he said his dad is at Dannemora."

Jared whistled.

"After my talk, the little guy asked me if I'd help him build a car for the Pinewood Derby."

"Are you going to?"

"Probably, after I talk with Ted Hazard, his Cub Scout Leader, and Owen's mother."

"Your job, Tessa's renovation, Hope's castle, this kid's Scout project and your volunteer fire department commitment. Think you might be spreading yourself a little thin?"

Josh stared at his older brother. "I can handle it."

Jared might have the money to throw around to help people, but he didn't have an exclusive on giving.

Chapter Three

The apartment was in worse shape than Tessa had expected. It looked like she had a good couple of hours' work clearing junk out before she even got to scrubbing off the years' worth of grime on everything. At least the appliances were in good condition, or they should be. Her grandmother had bought them from Jared and Becca last fall when they'd remodeled their kitchen, with the thought she might rent out the apartment.

She opened a box blocking the way from the kitchen to the living room. A combination of dust and mold tickled her nose. "Achoo!"

"God bless you."

Tessa spun around. "Josh, what are you doing here?"

"I had to pick up a few things at the grocery store, so I thought I'd swing by and see my new place." He weaved his way around the boxes and crates into the living room and peered into the bedroom. "Not much room for my furniture."

"Funny. When Grandma and Grandpa had the attic in the house insulated and sealed off to cut their heating costs, they moved everything that had been in the attic up here."

Josh stood in the middle of the living room, the top of his head almost touching the swag light that dangled from a hook in the ceiling. "It has potential."

Tessa followed his gaze around the place. "You've been reading real estate ads again. Looking for another house to flip?"

"Not this summer, not with the work you want me to do on the theater. And Hope asked me to build her a castle in Jared's backyard."

"A castle?"

"A playhouse that looks like a castle—I checked. We're still working out the details. And..." He hesitated. "With my degree almost finished, I'm hoping to have a project manager position with GreenSpaces lined up somewhere else by the end of the year."

Although Tessa knew Josh's ambitions, the thought that he could be leaving the area in a few months knocked the wind out of her.

"Don't worry," he said. "I don't see anything coming along before we get the theater work done."

She sucked in a breath. "It's not that."

"Then what?"

Was the man that thick? "I've gotten used to having you around, irritating as you can be, especially since almost everyone else I know is coupled off now."

He walked across the room and tugged a piece of old wallpaper that was curling down from the ceiling. "You don't have to stay around here." Josh pulled the wallpaper off in a long strip. "Say the word, and I'll put out feelers for any civil engineering jobs with GreenSpaces, or elsewhere. I'm always looking."

"Yeah, I know." She pushed a couple of strands of hair that had fallen from her topknot out of her face.

It shouldn't bother her that he didn't say he'd miss her when he left. But it did.

"Want me to stick around…"

Yes.

"And give you a hand here this afternoon?"

Tessa laid her finger along the side of her face as if she was thinking deeply. "I could use your brawn to move stuff out to the Dumpster behind the theater."

"Ah, saving my brains for the paid project."

"Right. I wouldn't want to use them all up before I got my money's worth."

"Ha! There's not enough money in the US Mint to buy all my smarts. Where do you want me to start?"

She tapped her foot against the box she'd been opening when Josh arrived. "This box can go downstairs for the Dumpster. It says 'for library sale,' but I don't know what year. The books smell moldy. I'm sure no one would want them."

"Are they old? Maybe you could find collectors online looking to buy some of them."

Tessa usually appreciated Josh's creative ways of making a few extra dollars, but not today. The musty stale air of the apartment was giving her a headache, and everything Josh said or did bugged her.

Josh strode over and lifted the box. "Whew. Cancel that thought. I'll take this downstairs, out in the fresh air. You can open some windows. There's a nice breeze that will blow some of the smell out of here. We'll regroup when I come back."

She watched him heave the box to his shoulder and head back out. *Regroup.* Yeah, that's what she needed to do. She'd become too dependent on her friendship with Josh. It was enabling her to hang back and not try to establish other friendships.

Josh burst back into the apartment a couple of minutes later. "I'm back. Point me in the direction of the next thing you want trashed."

Several hours and countless boxes later, the natural light in the apartment was growing too dim to continue working. They'd stashed the things worth keeping in the crawl space storage area that ran behind one wall of the living room. Tessa didn't have a clue why they hadn't been put there in the first place. The rest was in the Majestic's Dumpster.

Tessa tossed her cleaning cloth on the kitchen counter. "We'd better call it a night before it gets too dark to find our way out. I'll call the power company tomorrow and have the electricity turned on."

"No, I'll put it in my name. I didn't expect the free rent agreement to include utilities, and…" He grinned, emphasizing the smudge of dirt on his cheek. "The contract doesn't include them."

"Since when are you such a stickler for rules?"

"Since my getting paid depends on your financial success. Don't want to cut into your seed money."

Her chest tightened. He didn't have faith in her. And if he, her best friend, didn't, who would?

"Hey, lose the long face. I'm teasing. If you have an extra key you can give me before I leave, I'll stop by after work tomorrow and see if I can open those two windows that are painted shut."

But tomorrow was the first Monday of the month, the evening Josh usually came over with pizza or Chinese to view promotion clips of upcoming movies so she could choose what to order. A hollow grew inside her. This was Josh. Of course, business would come before fun—and friendship?

She dug in her jeans pocket for her key ring. "Right here." Tessa wound the key off the ring.

He took the key. "I can't give you much other help finishing the cleanup here until next weekend. But don't worry about having the place ready for me to move in on Thursday. Connor said it would be fine for me to stay at the parsonage while he and Natalie are away."

"Sounds good."

"Then pack up whatever you're taking with you, and I'll drop you at the house."

"No, you go ahead. I'll walk. I need some time out in the fresh air to clear my head of the smell of Mr. Clean." *And of other things, like the fear that our business partnership isn't the brilliant idea I thought it was.*

Tessa pressed the latch to the front door of the house, only to find it locked. She'd forgotten that Grandma was going to dinner and then a musical prayer concert at the Camp Sonrise Conference Center Auditorium with Josh's grandparents and Marie Delacroix. After she unlocked the door and let herself in, she dropped into the closest chair. Maybe Josh was right. Maybe the theater was a lost cause, and she should start looking for an engineering job. Opportunities here were slim, though, and she hated to leave her grandmother alone.

She pushed herself out of the chair to see what she could rummage up for supper. Her grandmother's words about Mrs. Delacroix inviting her to share her house ran through her mind. Grandma wasn't alone. Her roots were here. She had friends here. Grandma didn't need Tessa living with her any more than her parents needed her at the mission in Lesotho or, self-pity crept in, Josh needed her presence in his life. He couldn't seem to be with her lately without telling her about how he was out of here as soon as he found the right job opportunity or that she should look for an engineering job somewhere else.

Tessa found a note written on ivory stationery bordered with lilies of the valley in her grandmother's perfect penmanship.

> *I defrosted the leftover beef stew if you want it for supper, and Edna brought over a strawberry-rhubarb pie made with fresh rhubarb from her garden. There's vanilla ice cream in the freezer. Love, G.*

Tessa pulled the container of stew from the refrigerator. If she knew Grandma was well settled with friends, she could look for a job, maybe in Saratoga Springs or Glens Falls. Glens Falls was within commuting distance, if not for the months of bad winter weather. Tessa opened the stew container, and her stomach lurched. But that would mean moving and operating the Majestic weekends only, even during the summer tourist season, or not at all. Wherever she went, she'd have to establish a whole new support system. She'd come to Schroon Lake nearly six years ago and was still working on fitting in. And this was the most comfortable place she'd ever lived.

She replaced the lid on the stew container. Pie and ice cream sounded like a better supper. It had three of the four major food groups—dairy, grain and fruits and vegetables. Her hand lingered on the container after she'd placed it back on the refrigerator shelf, her parents' frequent reprimand sounding in her head. *You have to set an example. You can't simply choose to do whatever you want.*

She should have the stew. What kind of meal was pie and ice cream? Tessa grabbed the pie and closed the refrigerator door. She could have whatever she wanted for supper. There was no one here to set an example of good eating habits for, and Grandma wouldn't say anything. She cut a large piece of pie and smothered it in ice cream. Her cell phone rang as she polished off the last bite. She checked the number, figuring it could be one of only three people. Grandma checking up on her. Her heart warmed. Josh. The warmth ticked up a degree. Or Uncle Bob, whom she would call back later, or tomorrow.

She didn't recognize the number. "Hello."

"Tessa, it's Maura."

Her Alcoholics Anonymous sponsor. "Oh, hi."

"I missed last week's meeting and wanted to give you my new home phone number. We moved into the house yesterday."

"Congratulations," Tessa said.

"Thanks. I've got my work cut out for me the next few days unpacking."

"Me, too. I'm getting the apartment above my grandmother's garage cleaned out to rent. No one's lived in it for years."

"Have fun with that. I wanted to invite you to our housewarming party weekend after next."

Tessa twisted her hair around her finger. "What day?"

"Saturday evening. Some of the others from the meeting are coming. You can bring a guest."

"It'll depend on whether I can get Myles to cover for me." Relief edged with guilt flowed through her. She was thankful for the excuse. She didn't know whom she'd bring except her grandmother. Josh didn't know about her addiction. His hard feelings for his father had made her afraid to tell him and jeopardize their friendship—an accommodation to fitting in, like her drinking had started out as an accommodation to fitting in at college. She'd also chosen AA meetings in other towns where she'd be less likely to run into anyone from church or from the movie theater. Another accommodation.

"I hope you can come. Everything going well?"

"Yes and no." Tessa told her about the loan for the theater, the contract with Josh for the work and his bomb that he expected to have a job somewhere else by the end of the year. "I don't know if it's the project and wanting so badly for it to work out or the thought of my good friend moving, but I'm unsettled." She dropped her voice. "I wanted a drink last night, for the first time in forever."

"You should have called me."

"It went away as quickly as it came, and my grandmother had something she wanted to talk with me about."

"You know what you have to do with your uncertainty," Maura said. "Give it up to God."

"I know. I'll get back to you about the housewarming."

"Great. Call if you do need anything, and I'll see you tomorrow at the meeting."

"I will. Bye."

Tessa set her phone down, folded her hands and rested her elbows on the table. "Lord, I know only You can control my life. Direct me away from the pull of my addiction. Help me to know and accept the things I can't change, like Josh's inevitable move away from here, from me. I fear that I've let myself become too dependent on our friendship, that I've exchanged one dependency for another and that my reliance on him could jeopardize my sobriety when he leaves. Guide me to depend on You, the one who is always there for all of us. I place myself in Your hands. Amen."

The fire siren went off at the same time Josh received the text. He drove directly to the Schroon Volunteer Fire Department hall, bypassing his original destination, the apartment above Tessa's grandmother's garage. A quick glance at the parking lot showed only one other vehicle. He turned off his truck and read the text. An accident on US Route 9, near Paradox Lake, with possible fire potential. An Essex County Sheriff's deputy was already on the scene.

Josh heard the wind-down of a motorcycle slowing and turned to see Emergency Medical Squad members Jon Hanlon, a local obstetrician, and his wife, Autumn, a midwife, pull in. With only him and one other firefighter here, he still had time to call Tessa and let her know that he probably wouldn't be over to work on the windows at the apartment tonight.

"Hi," Tessa said, picking up on the first ring. "You just caught me. I was about to put my phone on vibrate."

"Right. Monday night video clips."

Tessa always turned her ringtone off and made him do the same, so any calls or texts wouldn't interrupt their viewing. He'd forgotten all about their regular Monday date, or rather non-date, yesterday when he'd said he'd stop by the apartment tonight. Josh waited a second for her to ask him to join her.

"You headed over to the apartment?" she asked.

Josh tapped his fingers on the steering wheel. "No,

that's why I'm calling. I'm at the fire hall. There's been an accident on Route 9."

"I'll let you go, then. I have to run and meet Myles at the Majestic. He's interested in learning how I choose the movies to show."

"Yeah, more people are pulling in. I've got to go. I'll see about the windows tomorrow night."

"Sure, whenever you get to them. It's your place now. Bye."

Josh slammed the truck door behind him. There was no logical reason Tessa watching the video clips with Myles should bother him. He'd encouraged Tessa to make more friends since his plan was to move up the ranks at GreenSpaces somewhere else. But Myles was a kid, a college student, not really their contemporary. Josh strode across the parking lot and into the fire hall. Tom Hill, the fire chief and owner of a car repair shop in Paradox Lake, and his son, Jack, were already suited up.

"Hey, Josh," Tom said, raising his hand to someone behind him. Jon and Autumn walked by them to the EMS vehicle.

"Grab your gear. It looks like we have enough volunteers now to take the tanker up."

His brother Connor's new father-in-law and brother-in-law had come in behind the Hanlons. With so many members working in Ticonderoga and other surrounding villages, getting a crew together could be hard.

Jack took his position behind the wheel of the truck while Josh and the others put on their protective gear. Tom pressed the button to open the hall door, and Jon and Autumn went ahead in the emergency vehicle followed by Tom in his pickup.

Josh and the other guys piled into the truck. Adrenaline rushed through him as the siren screamed and the lights flashed, increased by the fear he had whenever they responded to an accident that someone he knew might be involved.

He spotted the flashing lights of the sheriff car and the EMS vehicle when the fire truck raced through the intersection of Routes 9 and 74. Jack pulled the truck ahead of one of the accident vehicles, a pickup truck with a smashed left fender sprawled diagonally across the two lanes of the highway. The wrecker from Hill's Garage was already there, along with one from a garage in Schroon Lake. But Josh didn't see a second vehicle. He hopped off the truck and saw it, a compact station wagon with a crushed top rolled off the road in a small gully, resting against a stand of pine trees. A second emergency vehicle arrived from Newcomb as Jon and Autumn carried a stretcher down the incline.

Tom returned from talking with the deputy who was directing traffic. "A woman and two kids. Doesn't look good. The other driver is intoxicated." Tom jerked his head toward the deputy's car, where a middle-aged man sat staring out the window.

Bile choked Josh. The unkempt dark hair and strong profile reminded him of his father. He turned away and caught his breath. It wasn't him. Dad was dead, had been for nine years.

"Let's get the hose and extinguishers down there. The jaws of life, too," Tom commanded.

Josh joined his fellow volunteers, glad for the action to stop his thoughts. When he and the rest of the team reached the car, Jon and Autumn had a small unconscious form on the stretcher. He swallowed hard. The child looked about Hope's age, maybe a little younger.

The child's eyes opened. "Mommy?"

"We're working on getting her out," Autumn reassured him.

"There's a woman and another child trapped inside," Jon reported to Tom. "We talked to the little boy. The woman is unresponsive. Moriah and Newcomb are on their way."

"Newcomb's here," Tom said. "Pulled in right after us."

As if on cue, the second emergency squad came down the bank.

"We'll get this little guy up," Jon said. "I don't like the looks of that smoke from the engine, not with all the dead winter growth."

"That's why we're here," Tom said. "Jack, Donnelly." He motioned to the front of the car, and Josh and Jack began soaking it.

The third emergency squad arrived as Josh and the other firefighters were tramping back up to the road.

Tom approached the deputy when they reached the pavement. "If you want to get *him* to county lockup—" he jerked his thumb toward the deputy's car "—we can take over traffic control."

Josh made a furtive glance toward the car. The man had his head down, chin resting on his chest. *It couldn't be Dad.* He looked away. One wrecker had removed the pickup, and he could hear the fading siren of the Schroon EMS team on its way to the hospital. Hill's truck waited to take the car. Soon after, the other two rescue squads had extricated the woman and other child and taken off for the hospital.

"You guys can head back to the fire hall," Tom said. "I'll go back to the shop with the wrecker."

"The guy in the cruiser," Josh said. "Anyone we know?"

Tom shook his head. "The deputy said he didn't have any ID."

Josh wiped his forearm across his forehead. Responding to accidents always took more out of him than the actual physical demands warranted. He looked at the evening sky. If it wasn't too late, maybe he'd stop by the Majestic and hang out with Tessa and Myles. The drunk in the deputy's car and the little boy on the stretcher were juxtaposed in his mind. He could use some companionship to take the edge off before going back to the empty cabin.

His cell phone buzzed as he walked to the truck. It could be Tessa. He stopped and checked the phone. Connor's, not Tessa's, name flashed at him. Two missed calls and a text. His little brother was on his honeymoon. What could he want?

Josh swiped his finger across the screen and went stock-still when he read the text.

Call me. We got back from the beach, and there was a voice-mail message on my cell, forwarded from the parsonage phone. From Dad.

Chapter Four

Josh stared blankly at the phone screen. The colors of his apps blurred together. He shook his vision clear and jammed the phone back in his pocket. *Dear old Dad.* He had no doubt the call Connor had gotten was from their father. It fit his MO. Reappear after a bender expecting the family to welcome him home as if nothing had happened. Except this bender had lasted nine years. Dad had known better than to call him or Jared. He'd called Connor because Connor was a minister and most like their mother, making him the only one of them likely to take the call.

Josh grabbed the door handle and hurled himself into the back of the fire truck, looking over at the cleared accident scene. Bile rose in his throat as he focused his mind on the glimpse he'd had of the man in the sheriff's car. Once they were back at the firehouse and he called Connor, the first thing he was going to ask was when his father had called and from where. His skin tightened. If it was his father, it wouldn't be the first time he'd hurt someone driving drunk. Only this time it was kids.

"You all right, Josh?" Paul Delacroix, Connor's brother-in-law, asked.

Josh blinked Paul and the other guys in the truck into focus. "Yeah."

"Kids," Paul's father said. "I hate responding to injury accidents, but it's always worse when kids are involved."

"Right," Josh said. *And not only in car accidents.*

When they got to the firehouse, Josh took his time stowing his equipment. Now he sat in his pickup in the parking lot, his finger hovering over Connor's call notice on his phone screen. He touched it and pressed the phone to his ear.

"Hey, Josh," Connor answered.

"Hope I'm not interrupting anything."

Connor laughed. "No, we just got back from supper."

"So, was it really him?" Josh refused to personalize the man by calling him Dad.

"Yeah, it was Dad."

"You're saying that from the message he left, or you got back to him?"

"I called him back before we went to dinner."

"And he was drunk."

"He didn't sound drunk, wasn't slurring his words."

That didn't mean he hadn't been impaired enough to hurt that family.

"Dad called to—"

Josh clenched his free fist. How could Connor sound so calm about this? "I have a good idea why he called."

"He—"

Josh cut Connor off again. "What time did he call and when did you call him back?" Connor had probably called when their father was in the sheriff car and still had his cell phone, before the deputy had taken him to

Elizabethtown and booked him. "Where did he say he was calling from?"

"Back off. Do you want to know what he said or not?"

"I'd like the answers to my questions. When you called and texted me, I was responding to an accident caused by a drunk driver. A woman and two kids hurt. When we got there, the sheriff's deputy already had the other driver in his car. From his profile, the driver could have been the old man."

"The woman, the kids, do you know who they are?"

"No, only that one of the kids looked about Hope's age. The rescue squads took them to Glens Falls Hospital. Tom Hill probably knows."

"I'll call him later. As for Dad, he left the message this afternoon. I called him back about five-thirty at the Super 8 in Ticonderoga."

The original call had been too early to be the old man calling for Connor to bail him out of the DWI. But the callback was in line with the accident before the deputy had left. "That's what he told you, he was at the Super 8?"

"No, the number he called from that I called back was the Super 8. I did a reverse phone number lookup before I called."

Josh rubbed the back of his neck as some of the anger drained out of him. The man who'd caused the accident this evening couldn't have been their father. "Where's he been and what does he want?"

"All over the country. California mostly. He said being homeless was a lot more comfortable in San Diego than in Plattsburg."

"I'm supposed to feel sorry for him? He had a home here."

"No. He's in a twelve-step program and wants to make amends to us."

"I don't believe that for a minute. I wonder what he really wants out of us."

"He said he went down to Pennsylvania and talked with Mom."

Josh shook his head. "Unbelievable that he could show his face to Mom after everything he put her through, including dropping off the face of the earth and letting her think he was dead. Did you call her? He was probably looking for his share of money from her selling the house in Paradox Lake, the one she wore herself out working at the diner to pay for."

"I didn't talk with Mom, but I did talk with Jared. He and I both know alcoholics who are successfully working a twelve-step program, me through my counseling and one of Jared's close friends on the motocross circuit."

Sure, they're successfully working a program—a program of fooling everyone around them.

"Jared agrees with me that we should meet with Dad and hear him out."

"Big brother says so, so we should all fall in line. Well, count me out of your little family reunion. And don't give the old man my phone number."

"I wouldn't without your permission."

"You're not going to get it. Tell Natalie hello from me, and enjoy the rest of your honeymoon." Josh hung up without waiting for a response from his brother.

Josh gunned the engine of his truck and threw gravel as he tore out of the parking lot. By the time he'd reached the stop sign at the corner, he'd gotten control over himself. Leave it to their father to reappear just as he and his brothers were all doing well and were accepted by the locals who'd either scorned them or pitied them when they were growing up. That was probably it. Dad had gotten wind of their collective success and wanted to cash in on it. He turned left on US Route 9. Might as well follow his original plan and go to the apartment, use his excess adrenaline to unstick those windows. Then he could stop off at the Majestic if he saw the lights on there. His stomach grumbled. If Tessa hadn't ordered pizza for her and Myles, he would when he got there.

Yeah, that was what he needed to put the evening behind him. To hang out and watch some flicks with his best bud. Tessa would understand. She always did. He couldn't believe Connor and Jared, Jared especially, were giving in to their father. Josh wasn't about to be sucked in. There was no such thing as a recovering alcoholic.

Tessa started a clip from a new Disney film that had gotten good reviews as a film kids and adults could both enjoy.

"Disney?" Myles said. "I thought you wanted to increase attendance."

"Give it a minute. You haven't even seen the opening yet." Myles hadn't been anywhere near as objective judging the movies as Josh was, favoring blow-'em-up action adventures and panning everything else. While Josh liked thrillers and action-adventure films, he wasn't big on gratuitous violence. He'd said seeing gunfire firsthand took the attraction out of it. That was about the only thing he ever said to her about his tour in Afghanistan.

As the clip ended and Tessa marked the film as a

"yes," she heard what sounded like footsteps on the stairs to the projector room.

She tensed. "I locked the theater door, didn't I?"

"You did." Myles's mouth tightened into a thin line.

So it hadn't been her imagination. He'd heard the steps, too. Night noises never made her edgy when she and Josh were viewing clips. Tessa glanced sideways at Myles. She'd seen Myles grow from a teen into a young adult since she'd moved to Schroon Lake but still thought of him as Jamie Payton's oldest kid, all six-foot-one, and hundred and eighty-five pounds of him.

"I'll get the lock on the room door," he said. "You get ready to call 911."

The door swung open as Myles rose, and Tessa clenched the arms of her chair.

"Hey," Josh said. "Got any pizza left?"

Her heart dropped back from her throat to her chest. She hadn't thought about Josh and that he had a key for times when he worked late and stopped by after she'd already started viewing the clips.

"Um, I finished the last piece," Myles said. "I'll run out to the diner and get you something if you want, like if you guys want to be alone."

"Good idea." Josh pulled a few bills from his wallet. "Ask for my usual burger and fries. They'll know. And something to drink. Take your time."

Myles pocketed the money and grinned at Josh.

"Why did you do that?" Tessa asked.

"I'm hungry. With the accident and fixing the windows at the apartment, I didn't catch any supper."

Tessa crumpled the napkin on the table next to her and tossed it at Josh. "Not the food. The *take your time*. You're giving Myles the wrong idea about us."

"Hey, I have a reputation to uphold. I'm with a beautiful woman. What man wouldn't want her all to himself?"

Tessa warmed at his compliment while she also weighed whether to pick up her paper plate and chuck it at him. "As big an honor as it may be, I'd rather not join the long list of Josh Donnelly's former girlfriends. I prefer being on the more exclusive just-friends list."

"And you're at the top of that one. So what's wrong with my wanting to have you to myself for a few minutes? This is our usual Monday evening."

Tessa attributed the uptick in her heart rate to residual *ah* from the heartwarming romantic comedy clip she and Myles had watched before the Disney one. After all, this was good old love-'em-and-leave-'em Josh. No one she could take seriously.

"Do you have any clips left to view?"

"A couple." Tessa ran the videos and they talked about the films. She added them to her show list and shared the titles of the others she was ordering.

When Josh finished reading and commenting on her choices, he ran his hand over his hair and glanced around the room as if making sure they were really alone. "I've got some news."

"About the accident? Someone we know?"

Josh dropped into the chair beside her, where Myles had been sitting. "About my—"

"Yo, incoming food." Myles stomped up the stairs like half a detachment. "I've got your food." He inched the door open. "Didn't want to walk in on anything."

"Get in here. There was nothing to walk in on." Tessa glared at Josh.

"Yeah, right. I know that." Myles gave Josh a nod that she was sure he didn't think she caught. He handed Josh his food and fumbled for the change.

"Keep it for gas," Josh said.

"Thanks. Tessa, you don't mind if I leave now that Josh is here?"

An inexplicable wave of apprehension almost made her urge Myles to stay.

Myles cleared his throat. "A friend. You guys know her from church. Kaitlyn Flynn. She lives with Jack and Suzi Hill. She's in my algebra class at the college. She texted me for some help with our assignment. The Hills' house is on my way home. If I leave now, it won't be too late to stop."

Tessa was pretty sure she'd never heard Myles string together that many words about himself in one conversation. "Go ahead. I've showed you how I judge and choose the movies. That's what you wanted."

"Yeah. I'll come in early on Friday to be here for the candy delivery."

"That would be great." Tessa pinched her lips and held her breath until she heard Myles's last footfall on the stairs. Then she broke out in laughter. "Poor boy. From what Suzi told me, their former foster child Kaitlyn is a math whiz."

"So her call for help was all a setup." He joined in Tessa's laughter. "I should warn him."

"And break his heart? What guy doesn't want to be the white knight riding in on his trusty steed—in this case, math skills—to save the damsel in distress?"

"True. But some of us have more finessed rescue skills."

"You've never been watching from the outside."

He grinned. "So that's what you do, watch my moves?"

His tease hit a little too close to the mark. Sad as it sounded to her, she did watch him with other women, wondering when he'd start dating someone and have less time for her. Another sign she was too dependent on their friendship.

"Who could miss them? But get serious. Before Myles got back with your food, you said you had news."

Josh unwrapped his burger and lifted the roll. "Catsup, mustard, pickle. Good. They didn't forget the mustard."

Sometimes Josh was as reticent in his communication as Myles. "That's the news, the diner puts catsup, mustard and pickles on its burgers?"

He lifted his pointer finger while he finished chewing the bite he'd taken of the sandwich. His throat muscles worked as he swallowed. "Connor got a phone call from our father today." His jaw hardened. Josh placed the burger on its wrapper on the table.

"How?"

"The call was forwarded from the parsonage phone."

"I didn't mean that. I don't understand. Your father's dead."

"Don't I wish, but apparently not."

"Josh! You can't mean that." He'd shared bits and pieces with her of his growing up with his alcoholic father, probably more than he'd intended. It wasn't a pretty story, but she couldn't believe Josh would prefer his father dead if there was a possibility he was still alive. Or maybe she didn't want him to have that much hatred for his *alcoholic* father.

He dropped his chin to his chest. "I suppose not." He lifted his head, eyes blazing. "Apparently, he's here to make amends to us. But I don't have to want him here, want him messing up my life again."

Tessa scratched at a nick in her fingernail, thinking where she might be if her grandparents had felt the same way, if they and others hadn't accepted her apology, hadn't forgiven her. She swiveled her chair to face him directly, knee-to-knee. The play of anger and raw emotion on his face twisted her insides.

"I'm here, listening."

"I know." His voice was gravelly. "You always do."

His lopsided attempt at a grin pierced her heart. "Tell me what's going on."

"We never had concrete proof that my father was dead. We heard from him off and on for a while after he left and then nothing. Mom filed a missing person report. The last time anyone saw him was more than nine years ago, around the time Hope was born. According to the police report, he staggered out of a bar in Saranac Lake and disappeared, leaving his old truck in the parking lot. It was the middle of winter. Anything could have happened to him."

She shivered at the thought of what could happen to someone passed out in the woods on a sub-zero Adirondack winter night. Josh spoke with such detachment, as if commenting on something he'd heard on the news, rather than someone in his family, someone Tessa suspected Josh loved in the deepest recesses of his heart.

"Neither the police nor the private detective Jared hired for Mom found a trace of him after that. Until now." He puckered his mouth as if trying to get rid of a bad taste.

"So you all assumed he was dead? I don't think I could accept a family member's death without proof."

"You don't know my father."

She didn't know his father. But she knew people—men and women—like him, or like he was. Some of them were friends. One was her AA sponsor.

"Mom may have harbored a small hope that he was alive. But a couple of years ago when she wanted to sell the house in Paradox Lake and buy a condo near my aunt in Pennsylvania, she had to have him declared legally dead. It's been nine years since anyone has seen or heard from him."

He stood and began pacing the room, making Tessa wonder if his mother wasn't the only one who'd held open the thought that Jerry Donnelly wasn't dead. In Josh's case, though, it may have been fear he was still alive.

"My father's name was on the deed to the house, although I can't think that he ever contributed a thing toward it in money or keeping it up. His style was more trashing the place. My guess is that's why he showed up. Somehow he got wind that Mom sold the house and he wants his half of the proceeds to drink away."

Josh stopped at the other side of the room, back to her, facing the wall, and Tessa waited for him to continue.

The silence grew too loud for her. "So why's he here? The house sale is between him and your mother. It doesn't involve you guys." Tessa counted her heartbeats as she waited for Josh to answer.

"He's already visited Mom."

"Have you or your brothers talked with her?"

Josh picked up the pacing again.

"Can you sit?"

He stopped by the chair. "I don't know."

"You don't know whether your brothers have talked with your mother or whether you can sit?"

"Both. When I talked with Connor, they hadn't." He lowered himself into the chair and tapped his foot. "I'm certainly not going to be the first to call her. I'm not sure what I'd do if she's caved to him as usual and given him money." He blew out a breath. "Or worse, said she'd take him back. Since Mom moved to Pennsylvania, she's been happier than I ever remember her being."

Tessa studied Josh's rugged profile, choosing and discarding words in her mind. There was no way to step around the ones she needed to say. "You said your father wanted to make amends."

He jerked his focus toward her. "That's what he told Connor."

As if words could make up for what the old man had done to Mom and him and his brothers. He ran his gaze over Tessa's open face. What he'd done to his ability to have any kind of lasting relationship with a woman beyond his friendship with Tessa. What his father's parenting had done to any thoughts he ever might have entertained about having children of his own.

"It sounds to me like he's working a twelve-step program, like AA. Can you consider that maybe he's not drinking and does want to make amends?"

"Dear old Dad is always working something. As for him not drinking, once a drunk, always a drunk, no matter how you try to dress it up with programs."

While she should have been prepared, his words knocked the breath out of her. She reached for Josh's arm, and he jumped from the chair, opening a hollow space in her chest.

"Sorry. I need to go. I have to get some air. Maybe I'll swing by for the movie Friday night."

Tessa couldn't remember the last time Josh hadn't shown up on Friday night to help her show the weekly feature. "Wait. I'm done for the night. I'll walk down with you."

Josh held the door for her, tension radiating from him. When they got downstairs to the main door, she asked, "Will you consider what I said about your father making amends?"

He turned on her, his mouth drawn in a grim line. "No more questions. All I know is that I don't need any drunks in my life."

Tessa scrubbed the grout between the tiles surrounding the bathtub at the garage apartment as if her life depended on it being sparkling white. Josh hadn't stopped by the Majestic for the Friday or Saturday evening shows or the Sunday matinee. Nor had he sat with her and her grandmother at Sunday morning church service as he often did. In fact, if he was at church at all, he must have sat in the back and left before she and Grandma made it up the aisle.

But that's what she wanted, wasn't it, to be less dependent on Josh's friendship? His avoidance could be God's way of weaning her, which was why she hadn't contacted him since she'd seen him last Monday. But that didn't mean he wasn't on her mind. Constantly. Sunday evening on her way home from work, she'd checked the apartment to see if he'd been there. He was supposed to be moved in, except they'd never finished the cleaning. She'd found new boxes on the living room floor, air fresheners plugged in a few of the electrical sockets and the carpeting no longer had the muddy look the several years' accumulation of dust had given it.

She sprayed more cleaner on the wall. So what had she done? Instead of texting or calling Josh to get together to finish the cleaning, she'd come over to the apartment late the past three afternoons and cleaned, thinking Josh might stop in after work. *Pitiful.* She needed to get a life, which was what she'd been trying to do with the Majestic renovations, and redirect her relationship with Josh to a working one. She didn't need the grief of getting in the middle of him and his father. Josh needed to work that out himself.

The click of the apartment door opening made her drop the scrub brush in the tub. It landed with a thud that echoed through the apartment. The only people who had keys besides her were her grandmother and Josh, and Josh would be at work.

"Hello, what brings you up here?" she called to her grandmother, rising and walking to the doorway to the main room.

Josh and Claire Delacroix stood by the entry door. "I didn't expect you to be here," he said.

"Why aren't you at work?" she blurted. *And why is Claire with you?* "I mean, I thought I'd finish the cleaning." She dug the toe of her sneaker into the corner of the doorjamb. As of last Thursday, the apartment was his. She was the one who didn't belong here.

"I appreciate it, but I was caught up at work for the moment, so took off a couple of hours this afternoon to move. I didn't get it all done over the weekend."

Right, because the only time you had was the hours I was working and you knew you wouldn't run in to me.

"I can finish. You've got better things to do than clean my apartment," he said.

Of course he could finish—him and Claire. "Sure, I'll get my stuff. There's not much left to do." She went back into the bathroom. What was with her? She never got tongue-tied and uneasy with Josh. Nor did she pay particular attention to who he was seeing, except to bust on him. Tessa dumped the dirty cleaning water in the tub and watched the grime spiral down the drain before she rinsed the tub and her bucket. Pasting a smile on her face, she crossed the main room to the door where Josh and Claire were still standing.

"Have fun," she said, pulling the door open. "And Josh, once you're settled in, text me about when you can get started with the work at the Majestic."

"Wait," Claire said, grabbing the door as Tessa pulled it closed. "I'm here to see you. I couldn't get you on your cell phone. I stopped by the house, and your grandmother said you were here. I ran into Josh on the walk over."

Tessa released the door handle. "Oh, I thought..."

Or, rather, she hadn't thought. She'd reacted. She and Claire had had lunch together yesterday when Tessa was shopping in Ticonderoga near Claire's satellite work office. Lunch had been a spur of the moment idea Tessa had had to expand her friendships beyond Josh. Claire had spent the whole time talking about Nick, a guy she'd recently started seeing.

"Never mind. What's up?"

Claire stared at her. "You thought I was here with Josh, to help him move in?" She laughed. "And I thought you knew me."

Tessa shook her head. "Yes, what was I thinking?"

"Hey." Josh waved his hand in front of them. "I'm right here."

She patted him on the shoulder. "We know. We're your friends. We're keeping you from becoming too self-important. So, back to why you're looking for me, Claire."

"What we talked about at lunch yesterday." Claire glanced at Josh and back.

Tessa's mind blanked.

"Me, Nick, his cousin. Remember, I told you that when I talked Nick into the Resurrection Light concert a week from Friday, he bought tickets for his cousin and a date." Claire twisted a lock of her hair. "Safety in numbers. I don't know about his cousin, but Nick's not really a practicing Christian. I have hopes, though."

Equal measures of guilt about forgetting and compassion for Claire's hopes filled Tessa as she recalled their lunch conversation.

"You were going to let me know today if you had someone to handle the concessions at the Majestic, so Myles could cover for you in the projector room," Claire said.

"Let me see if I can help," Josh said, grinning. "Claire's setting you up, or trying to set you up, with a date for the concert. Have I got that right, Claire?"

"Nothing gets by you."

"I can collect tickets and manage the concession stand for Friday. Or run the movie," Josh said.

"You aren't going to the concert?"

"No, don't you remember? I waited too long to get tickets and they were sold out." Josh crossed his arms over his chest.

She shook her head. He sounded almost hurt, as if she should remember.

"Yeah, Myles said his mom and Eli were going. She's a huge fan. He asked if he could bring his sisters to watch the movie while he worked, so Jamie and Eli wouldn't have to get a sitter for them."

"I remember Myles asking about Rose and Opal. They'd love to see the movie from the projector room."

Josh frowned. "I said we should go to the concert, too. That I'd check on getting tickets."

"Wait. Wasn't that when Myles was putting a new CO_2 container in the soft drink machine and Pepsi spewed out all over him? I guess what you said didn't register."

Why was he making such a big deal? Was he that disappointed about missing the concert? Her pulse ticked up. Or was he bothered that she'd forgotten he'd suggested they go and now she was going with Claire and her friends? If she decided to go. She wanted to cool her friendship with Josh, not kill it.

"Maybe you could buy Claire's friend's extra ticket. The theater's my responsibility, not yours, and I only work the three days."

Josh's frown transferred to Claire's face. *Another disgruntled friend.* She was losing what social skills she'd thought she'd developed, and fast.

"You'd give up your concert ticket for me?" Josh uncrossed his arms, placed his hands over his heart and lifted his chin. "Now that's friendship. But you don't get out of the first date you've agreed to in months that easily."

"I hadn't agreed." Tessa pushed a stray strand of hair off her face and dropped her gaze to the floor. The teasing was more Josh, but he was still acting weird.

"Sure you had. Right, Claire?"

"I thought so."

"It's settled. I'll fill in for Myles Saturday, so he can show the movie and you can go out with Claire and her friends."

"Works for me," Claire said. "I'll get in touch with the details after I talk with Nick." She checked her watch. "I'd better get back to work."

"Yeah, it'll be fun," Tessa said, remembering how excited Claire had been at lunch yesterday when she'd invited her to the concert.

The door closed behind Claire. "Why do I feel like

I did in high school when my other grandmother in Batavia told one of her friends that I needed a date to the Spring Fling, and the friend said her son, the class clown, would be happy to take me? I could have had a date if I'd wanted one. But I hadn't, and certainly not with him. I'd planned to study for the SATs with another friend that weekend."

Josh shrugged. "You'd planned to spend a Saturday night studying?"

"My friend was really nervous about the test. It was the only evening we both had free before we were scheduled to take it."

"That's why Claire and I had to step in."

"What are you talking about?"

"Sit down." He directed her to the couch. "It's okay. I aired out the cushions Sunday morning and vacuumed the rest of it."

So he hadn't been at church. He'd been avoiding her. She sat and tried to find a comfortable spot between the lumps and springs. "You might want to get a new couch."

"Stay on topic. Sometimes, you're too responsible."

Being responsible worked for her. Moving to Schroon Lake and taking over the movie theater had gotten her away from the dark pit she'd crawled out of and helped her stay sober. "But I only work Friday and Saturday nights and Sunday afternoons."

"And spend the other four days working on the details of the renovations, that is, until we begin the actual renovations. Then you'll be spending the other four days working on the renovations. Claire and I did you a favor making your decision for you."

"You didn't make my decision. I was going to say yes anyway after I realized how much it means to Claire."

A two-second study of Josh's face showed none of the disappointment or jealousy she'd obviously imagined a few minutes ago. He had his brothers and guy friends and girl friends. He wouldn't care if she hung out with Claire and Nick.

He caught her lingering gaze and the corner of his mouth turned up. "Great."

Her heart shrank. Now he had her wondering if she'd been trying too hard, smothering him in friendship. She'd done it before.

"Now," he said, "I need a favor in return." He nudged a box by the door with the toe of his work boot. "I trust your judgment."

"Thanks. Now, your judgment sometimes…" She couldn't help teasing. His expression had turned so serious, so un-Josh-like, that it unsettled her more. She needed to restore her equilibrium.

"Hey," he said.

"I'm kidding. What's up? A job opening?" She bit her lip and reached deep inside herself for the happiness she should feel for Josh if a work opportunity he wanted was in reach.

"No, it's about my father."

Her gut twisted. She wasn't getting involved with him and his father.

"Jared and Connor are hounding me about going with them to see him."

Her heart leaped with hope. Josh's voice held far less anger than last week.

"You really think I should go hear him out?"

All the hope seeped out. Josh needed to make this decision himself. It was far bigger than her agreeing to a blind date. He shouldn't depend on her to tell him what to do, no matter how strongly she felt he should meet with his father. Tessa clenched her hands, digging her fingernails into her palms. Her opinion was biased and selfish, and nothing good could come of sharing it with Josh. But she shared it anyway.

"Yes, I think you should hear your father out."

Chapter Five

Josh rammed his truck into second gear and tore onto the highway. Why had he let Tessa talk him into seeing his father? He gunned the gas, skipped from third to fifth gear and flew around the curve toward Ticonderoga to see a flashing sheriff's car with someone pulled over to the right. He tapped the brake to slow down to the fifty-five-mile-an-hour speed limit and adjusted his shades. Who was he kidding? Tessa hadn't talked him into anything. He'd asked her opinion and she'd given it, straight out, as she always did, whether she thought he'd like it or not. He'd made the decision to come, a decision he was regretting more with each mile he drove.

He cruised into Ticonderoga, welcoming the slower speed limit at the village line. The time on the bicentennial clock on Montcalm matched the time on the dashboard clock, six-forty, twenty minutes early for the meeting, with only five minutes' distance to cover. He refused to be the first one there. A coffee shop sign beckoned him, causing his stomach to alternately growl and clench. He hadn't eaten, couldn't face the old man on a full belly, and had downed the last of the hours old office coffee before he'd left work.

His father had done it again. Had him walking on eggshells. His queasiness had nothing to do with the stale coffee. Dear old Dad had reduced him to his teen-age self, guts churning as his friend Marc Delacroix, Claire's twin, approached the house to drop him off after school. Never knowing what he'd find when he went in. Hoping he could clean up any mess before the school bus got there with Connor.

Josh jerked the truck into the motel lot and parked, looking around for Jared's truck or bike and Connor's car. When he didn't see either, he reached for his phone. He could use a pep talk from Tessa. The time glared at him. Six forty-eight. Tessa would be at the Majestic ready to start the movie. He didn't need Tessa. He didn't need anyone. Old instincts took over. He got out of the truck and strode across the parking lot, swinging open the lobby doors and glancing around for the elevator or stairs.

"Welcome to the Super 8," the middle-aged woman behind the counter said. "Do you have a reservation?"

"No, I'm here to meet my fa—someone. Room 25." Why had he given the room number? *Easy.* To waste time. He rubbed the sweat from his neck at his hairline. *What a wuss.*

"Mr. Donnelly. He was just here talking to me on his way back from supper. What a charmer." She smiled and shook her head.

Dad certainly was, especially when he had a few drinks in him.

"Was he…never mind." He'd find out soon enough if he'd been drinking. Yeah, it was good that he'd gotten here before Connor, although he wouldn't mind having Jared as backup and a possible voice of reason. Jared had mellowed a lot since he'd married Becca and started working with the kids at his motocross school.

"The elevator, stairs?"

"To the left. Wait."

Josh stopped, nerves twitching. This was where the woman would tell him Dad's condition.

"You're one of his boys. I should have caught the resemblance."

He sucked the raw taste from his mouth, wanting to disagree. But unfortunately, he and Jared did look like their father.

"Are you the motocross champion, pastor or—"

"No, I'm the other one. You said to the left?"

"Yes. He's so looking forward to seeing you guys."

That made one of them. "Thanks, uh, for the help." Josh crossed the lobby in three long strides and stood out of the woman's sight in the hallway. He alternately pressed his fists together knuckle to knuckle in front of his chest and rolled his shoulders to get rid of the tension before he climbed the stairs to the second floor and his father's room. At the top, he heard the ding of the elevator and waited for the door to open. A couple stepped off and smiled at him as they headed to their room.

Heart thudding, Josh crossed the hall to room 25. He reached up and rapped the door twice, listening to the noises in the room for a drawer closing as his father stashed a bottle, feet shuffling, and holding his breath as he mentally counted the response time. The click of the door opening put him at attention.

"Joshua."

He bristled. No one but his mother called him Joshua.

"Come in," his father said in a voice uncomfortably close to his own.

Somehow, Dad seemed smaller than he remembered, although at twenty, Josh had been as tall as he was now. His hair was still thick and dark, except for a little white at the temples. He lacked the typical two days' growth on his square jaw, and the lines on his face were less pronounced.

"Let me take a look at you," his father said. "It's been a long time, since before you went to Afghanistan." He raised his hand as if expecting criticism from Josh. "My fault. I know. Have a seat."

Josh inventoried the room as he weighed whether that was an invitation or a command. Bath and queen-size bed on the door side. Desk, couch—probably a pull-out—and two chairs on the far side near the window.

"I need to hit the latrine first. Coffee ran right through me." Josh sniffed the air as he walked in front of his father. He didn't smell alcohol. In the bath, he quietly and efficiently inspected the cabinet under the counter— paper and cleaning supplies—and the tub behind the closed shower curtain for bottles. He smelled the glass on the sink back.

"Did I pass inspection?" his father asked when he returned.

Josh sat in one of the chairs and his father took the other one. "I don't care what you do."

"But you were watching out for Connor. Your mother told me that you used to try to get home from school and run interference for me before Connor got off the school bus. Thanks."

"I didn't do it for you," Josh said, shooting for a rise out of his father.

"I know. You did it for your brother. Your mother also told me you've been doing some house flipping. When we were first married, I used to do some of that."

He cracked his knuckles and got only a grimace from his father. Knuckle cracking had always been enough to set him off. Josh knew he was being juvenile, but he didn't care what the old man used to do or was doing now, for that matter, and he certainly didn't want to be compared to him. More than that, he couldn't take the cool, calm conversation. It fanned the small flame deep inside him that wanted his father to be sober, to have a normal relationship with him.

A sharp rap made them both turn toward the door. His father stood, crossed the room and looked out the peephole. Who would it be besides Jared or Connor? Or had he already hooked up with some of his old drinking buddies?

His dad opened the door. "Jared, Connor."

Jared offered his hand as he stepped in. "Dad."

Connor followed with his arms open. "Good to see you." He hugged him.

Hugged him. Connor sure was buying the amends, this whole recovering-alcoholic bit, lock, stock and barrel. Or maybe his baby brother had been too young to remember their father as anything but perpetually drunk. Josh and Jared remembered a dad who wasn't. He didn't know about Jared, but that made him even more resentful of what their father had become before he'd left them, what he still was as far as he was concerned.

"Come in, sit down. As you can see, Joshua is already here."

Jared raised an eyebrow, the action shouting to Josh, *here first? And I wasn't sure you'd even show up.*

"Yeah. We've been talking about old times." Josh pasted his best facsimile of a smile on his face before his older brother gave him and Dad the critical appraisal Josh expected.

"You guys want a drink?" his father asked.

Josh wasn't the only one who tensed. He hadn't been bold enough to check the small refrigerator by the bath.

His father didn't miss a beat. "Relax," he said as if he'd made the comment on purpose to get a rise out of them. Or out of him. "I've got ice tea and Cokes."

"Coke," Jared and Connor said.

"What kind of tea?" Josh snapped out.

"It's not hard, if that's what you're asking," his father said.

Josh didn't have to see his brothers' disapproval. The air crackled with it.

"No, I meant sweetened or unsweetened." Josh pressed his lips tight.

"Sweetened."

"I'll take tea."

His father got the drinks and passed them out.

"Thanks," Josh said, taking the frosty can and feeling his father's gaze on him as he looked at the alarm clock by the bed. He'd thought pulling out his phone to check the time would be too obvious.

"Sorry I got defensive about the drinks. I'm nervous," his father said.

"We all are," Jared assured him.

Josh figured challenging his brother's speaking for all of them wasn't in his best interest of getting out of there as quickly as possible.

Their father sat at the opposite end of the couch from Connor and crossed and uncrossed his ankle over his knee while he drummed the arm of the couch. "Like I said to you and Connor on the phone, as part of my program, I'm making amends to people I've hurt, wronged in the past. I saw your mother before I came back here and have been to court to have my death certificate rescinded. As a heads-up, your mother and I are going to divorce."

"Got someone in the wings?" Josh asked.

His father sank into the couch.

Josh couldn't stop himself. "And as a heads-up to you, you're a little late to make your amends to Hope's mother or her grandmother."

"I know." His father studied his hands in his lap.

"Lay off him, Josh," Connor said. "Let him talk."

Their father lifted his head. "I don't have anyone waiting in the wings," he said in a subdued voice. "But apparently your mother does." His father cleared his throat. "Seems like a good guy. I met him while I was in Pennsylvania. Don't let on that I told you. They're planning to share their news in person."

"Sorry, Dad," Connor said.

"Sorry about what?" Josh shot to his feet. "After everything he did to Mom, what do you expect?"

"You always were her champion," his father said.

"Someone had to be." He glared at his father and Jared. "You all seem to be on a different wavelength than me. I think it's time I go."

"Stay until I finish. Please. Everything you've said is right. That's why I'm here. I was a lousy husband and father."

Josh eased back into his seat and took a slug of his tea, sloughing off the fleeting thought that he might be nearly as dependent on caffeine as the old man was on booze.

"I can't change the past. I can't make up for what you missed and I missed when you were boys, although I thank the Lord for giving me another opportunity with Hope. Jared and I are going to work something out."

Hope. She's why Jared had talked with their father

before tonight. Josh pressed back into his chair. Jared wasn't totally abandoning their mutual distrust of their father by jumping on the New Jerry Donnelly bandwagon with two feet the way Connor had.

"I'd like to get to know you as men. From what I've heard around town you've grown to be pretty fine ones."

"Thanks to Mom," Josh added, in case his father was going to try to take any credit for the hard work it had taken all three of them to earn the respect they had in the community now as adults. Respect that would erode when their father fell off the wagon if he stuck around.

"Yes, all the credit goes to your mother and you guys. I'm not making excuses. I'm not expecting you to welcome me back with open arms, or even like me."

His father's gaze traveled around the circle, resting a moment longer on him than on Jared and Connor. Josh shifted in the chair.

"You may not be able to believe it, but I've always loved you boys in my own dysfunctional way. I'm trying to make a new sober life for myself, and I'd like you in it. What I'm asking is if we can try to put the past behind us and get to know each other as we are now. Then we can make our personal judgments."

Josh reached for his empty tea can on the low table between the chairs and the couch to avoid his father looking him in the eyes again.

"Would you like to pray on that?" Connor asked.

"Yes. And for the Lord to be with me tomorrow when I make my amends to Liz Whittan."

Dad sure was playing his amends thing up big time. Liz was the local schoolteacher he and his friend had smashed into and crippled while driving drunk when Josh was in middle school.

"Dad, you know Sheriff Norton came clean about

what really happened that night, that Bert Miller was driving, not you," Jared said.

"Yeah, he sent your mother a letter. Guess he was making amends, too."

"You probably could get reparation for the time you spent in jail for vehicular assault. It might help you make your new start," Jared said.

So Jared was buying their father's new start facade?

"The only one who deserves reparation is Liz, and all I can give her is my sincere apology."

"But you weren't driving," Connor said.

"I didn't stop Bert from driving. How about that prayer?" He reached across the couch for Connor's hand and toward the chair for Josh's.

He accepted his father's clammy hand and took Jared's, completing the prayer circle. Sure, he could pray with him and accept that his father was back in Paradox, maybe to stay. He couldn't do anything about where his father chose to live. But he didn't have to believe anything else dear old Dad said. He'd learned too well that believing in his father only set him up for disappointment, or worse.

Tessa looked up from her e-reader to check on the movie. Neither the movie nor her book, a fast-paced romantic suspense that she'd generally be devouring, held her attention. Showing movies was boring work when you didn't have any company. She checked the time on her phone, wondering if Josh and his brothers were still with their father and whether he'd let her know how it went. She'd been as noncommittal as she could be when he'd texted her this afternoon that he'd decided to go. The situation hit too close to home and weighed heavy on her conscience. Her grandmother wouldn't say anything to him, but what if he found out about her some other way? She stood and tried to stretch out some of the tension that was knotting her muscles. What she needed was a good run, but it would be too dark after the movie finished and she closed up.

The projection room door creaked open. "Out of Pepsi already?" she asked. "We must have a full house of thirsty moviegoers."

"I wouldn't know," Josh said.

Tessa dropped her arms. "Hey. I thought you were Myles enlisting my help to change the CO2 container in the soft drink dispenser. Having a second person around when changing them is a good idea, unless you like a soda bath."

"I remember."

"So, how did the crowd look?"

"I didn't check. I was too starved. I came in the back and right up with the food." He placed a pizza box on the table, threw open the top releasing the spicy scent of pepperoni and tomatoes and grabbed a piece before sitting down. "I didn't eat before I went to Ticonderoga."

Before I went to Ticonderoga, not *before I saw Dad* or *before we met with Dad.* Tessa's neck muscles reknotted. "How'd it go?" As if he hadn't already made the answer clear.

"I've accepted that he's back in Paradox Lake, and there's nothing I can do about it except make a concerted effort to avoid him."

She studied the stony set of his jaw as Josh motioned toward the pizza. "You going to have some?"

"In a minute." She clasped her hands to still the chill that ran through her despite the heat of the small, humid room. "What about Jared and Connor?"

"I can't read Jared clearly. He seems to be weighing

things because of Hope. Connor's lapping up all of his baloney about making amends, wanting to get to know us as men, ad nauseam." Josh tossed his half-finished slice on the open box top. "What does Connor need him for anyway? Jared and I are the ones who've been there for him."

Tessa reached over to pick up a piece of pizza she didn't want and to buy some time to calm the turmoil inside so he wouldn't see it on her face. "There's no way you can give your father the benefit of the doubt, give him time to show he's changed, before you shut him out?"

"No, why should I?"

Tessa jerked straight at his vehemence, almost dropping the pizza in her lap.

"You don't know what it's like," he said.

She knew more than he'd ever guess.

"He's not like us."

Tessa choked down the bite of pizza she'd taken. "Have you thought about checking out an Al-Anon meeting to help you deal with your father? People there would understand."

He glared at her. "No, I'm not sitting around spouting my personal business with a bunch of strangers."

"After you'd gone a few times, they wouldn't be strangers."

"Who made you such an expert?"

"I…" She checked out the time remaining in the movie, her heart pounding. "I had an experience in college." She breathed in and out. She should tell him, even if it meant a clean break in their friendship. That might be exactly what Josh needed to heal, and she needed to stop walking on eggshells and regain her serenity.

Josh grabbed his half-eaten slice of pizza and folded it in half. "Can we talk about something else? It's not as if I'm going to choose to see him while he hangs around here, which I expect won't be for long. And once GreenSpaces has an opening for a project manager and I'm out of here, I won't have to have anything to do with him." He crammed the slice in his mouth and took a bite.

"Yeah, sure." The moment had disappeared, along with her courage. "We can talk about something else."

She couldn't make Josh attend meetings, heal him and dispel his bitterness any more than Josh and his family could have made his father stop drinking. Only Josh and God had the power to heal him. She of all people knew that. Tessa clenched her jaw. She was falling into old patterns. Rather than distancing herself from Josh, as she'd decided to do, she was getting more involved in his life, being helpful so he'd like her.

He finished his pizza slice. "If you got the building permit today like you thought you would, I'm ready to start work on the renovations Monday night."

"I didn't get the permit." Tessa focused on the film as if she was checking on how long it had to go. "I ran an errand first, and when I got back to Schroon Lake, the building inspector had gone home sick and the clerk didn't know anything about the permit."

Her errand had been attending an extra meeting she knew her sponsor would be at. "I'll get the permit Monday and do what prep work I can during the day. I have plans for the evening."

A *choo choo* blasted from Josh's pocket. "One of the kids," he said, concentrating his full attention on retrieving his cell phone. "When Brendon turned eleven, Jared and Becca got him a phone, so he could call from sports practice and Boy Scouts for rides home. His sister and Hope think it's theirs, too."

After reading the text, he said, "Looks like I won't be available to work Monday evening after all. Hope's volunteered me to coach her soccer team, the one Hill's Garage sponsors. The person who was lined up to coach has taken a new job out of the area."

"I know."

He laughed, the sound lightening the atmosphere of the room. "You know what?"

"About the coach." Tessa paused and nodded. "And that you're going to tell Hope you'll do it."

"Ha! You're so into me that you can read my mind."

She slugged his shoulder to ward off the pall that was descending again.

"Ouch. What was that for?" He rubbed his arm.

"I'm into you? In your dreams."

He was in her dreams, only not in the way she'd implied to Josh. More like thoughts that kept her mind churning and her tossing and turning half the night.

"I know about the soccer coach because Suzi Hill called this afternoon and asked if I'd coach. She has a new foster kid on the team and had heard somewhere— had to be from my grandmother—that I'd played in college." At least she had before she'd messed up and lost her spot on the team. "And you never tell Hope no."

"You said yes to coaching, right?"

"I did. Suzi said the team has nearly as many girls as boys, and the former coach was really a husband-wife team."

"All right!" He raised his hand for a fist bump. "We can co-coach. Wait until I show them my moves. Look out, playoffs. The team will be unstoppable."

"Earth to Josh. We're talking second and third graders, not the US men's team."

"And they'll be playing other second and third graders. We'll cream them." He thumbed a message. "I texted Hope and Jack Hill."

He hadn't even asked if she wanted him to co-coach. Coaching the team had been part of her program to distance herself from Josh and spend more time with other people. A program she intended to work as hard as her AA program, and he wasn't making it any easier for her.

He got another *choo choo*, followed by a *ding*.

"Done. That was Jack. We're the new coaches of the Hazardtown Hornets."

His grin of pure joy, the first she'd seen since his father had reappeared, shot right to her heart, which didn't bode well for her distancing plan, either.

Chapter Six

"This is cool, isn't it Josh? Me playing soccer with my best friend, Sophia, and you coaching with your best friend, Tessa?" Hope jogged at Josh's side as they rounded the corner of the school toward the sports fields. He was twenty minutes late for his meet time with Tessa and ten late for the practice.

"Tessa is your best friend, right? You hang out with her all the time, and you said she's not your girlfriend."

Josh spotted Tessa handing out the kids' Hornet shirts and socks and waved. She was dressed in fitted soccer shorts and her official coach T-shirt with a Geneseo State hoodie over it. Her long, wavy hair was pulled back in a ponytail that hung through the hole in the back of her baseball cap. He was still in his business-casual work clothes.

"Well, is she?" Hope demanded.

"Is who, what?" He'd lost track of what Hope had been saying.

She huffed. "Is Tessa your best friend?"

What was it with Hope and him and Tessa being friends? "I guess, except for Jared and Connor."

Or maybe ahead of his brothers considering all she

put up with from him. "I've never thought about it." Tessa was Tessa, someone he liked being around and didn't have to impress.

"You don't have to think about it, you're just best friends, like me and Sophia," Hope said, using nine-year-old logic. "I don't think you're really best friends. You'd know."

But he didn't know and somehow that made him feel empty.

"Race you to the field," he said, giving her a twenty-yard lead before going all out to clear his head. Ten feet from the white line delineating the soccer field, Josh slowed his pace so Hope crossed a second before he did.

"And, here making a grand entrance is Coach Josh." With a flourish, Tessa motioned toward him. "Glad you could join us," she added for his ears only, as she handed him his clipboard with the team roster.

"I got tied up at work and had to pick up Hope. Jared's out of town and Becca's carting one of the other kids somewhere."

"I'm teasing." Tessa buddy-slapped him on the back.

The jolt that shot through him raised an awareness of the warmth, then coolness of the spot where her hand had touched him. He flexed his fingers, Hope's *I don't think you're really best friends* ringing in his head. If he and Tessa weren't friends, what were they?

"Most of the team played last year," Tessa said, "so I thought we'd scrimmage to see the kids' skills."

"Sounds good," he said. Tessa certainly had everything organized. He clapped his hands to get the kids' attention. "Okay, everyone line up." He watched as the twelve kids who'd showed up for practice scrambled to form a line in front of him and Tessa. "Now count off by fours."

Tessa tilted her head in question, making her pony-tail flop over her shoulder. She so rarely wore her hair down, he'd forgotten how long it was. A picture of her at Connor's wedding filled his mind. How pretty she'd looked with her hair curling around her face and down her back.

He cleared his throat. "You'll see. To mix up the teams."

Tessa nodded.

"Three, four," Hope and her friend Sophia finished the count off.

"All of the ones and fours, put on your Hornets T-shirts. You'll be on Tessa's 'shirts' team."

"Put them on over the shirt you have on," Tessa said. Most of the kids had on long-sleeved T-shirts or sweat-shirts.

"Twos and threes are on my 'flags' team," Josh said, automatically thinking of the pickup soccer games he and his high school friends played and the group of girls who used to come watch them. Had Tessa done that, watched her male classmates "perform" for the girls?

Hope skipped over. "What do you mean by our team being flags?"

"I'll give you guys bandannas to tuck in your back pocket or waistband and hang down."

Tessa handed him a package of bandannas she'd brought with the shirts.

He ripped the package open to shake off the irrational irritation that had come with the thought of Tessa watching other guys play soccer or anything else. *Get real, that would have been twelve or thirteen years ago.* Long before Josh had met her. He couldn't figure what was wrong with him. Tessa and other men had never both-ered him, not that she dated much. The other day he'd encouraged her to go to the concert with Claire's friend.

"All right," he said. "When I point to you, tell me your name, if you played soccer last year and what position if you did." Josh went down the roster familiarizing himself with the kids' names and experience and assigning them positions for the scrimmage. Since only twelve of the fourteen kids on the roster had showed up, he had no problem getting everyone in.

"You ready over there?" Tessa asked, her hands-on-hips stance emphasizing her trim build.

He tore his gaze away. "More than ready."

"Then let's get this game going." Tessa blew the whistle around her neck and the teams took their positions.

As he and Tessa raced up and down the sidelines refereeing and giving their teams directions, he found his attention jumping from the kids to Tessa, watching her move with unconscious athletic grace. He'd never noticed it before. He knew she liked sports, at least watching them with him on TV, and that she ran, but lots of women did to stay trim. How had he missed that she was an athlete? The better he thought he knew Tessa, the more she surprised him with new facets.

With his team one point behind, one of the players passed the ball to Hope near their goal. "That's it," he said, "aim."

The ball went flying over the net, just as the parent timekeeper yelled time.

"Yay!" Tessa's team shouted in victory and ran to her.

Ignoring Tessa's motion to the kids to join her on the other side of the field where their parents were sitting, Hope dragged herself over to Josh. "Sorry."

He put his arm around his sister's shoulders. "For what?"

"For making us lose the game. I could have tied it."

Josh squatted in front of her. "It was a practice, and

you didn't make us lose. There were five other players for your team on the field."

"But I had the ball and I could have made a goal if I didn't kick it so hard."

"So now you know how hard to kick the ball when we're playing a real game. That's what practices are for."

"I guess."

He stood and squeezed her shoulder. "That's my girl. Come on. We need to hear what Tessa is saying or we won't know what's going on."

"Don't you already know? You're the coach, too."

"So they tell me."

"You're funny, Josh." Hope pulled him across the field.

"So, we'll see you all Wednesday at five-thirty," Tessa said. "Only one more practice before opening day on Saturday."

The kids and their parents streamed off toward the parking lot, except for Jack Hill and a boy kicking a soccer ball down the sideline. *Had to be Jack and Suzi's new foster child.*

"I don't see Becca," Hope said, an anxious note creeping into her voice.

"She must be running late. I'll text her. She can pick you up at my place." Josh sent the text and grimaced. Although Hope had come a long way since she'd lost her maternal grandmother who'd cared for her most of her life, and come to live with Jared and Becca, she still had abandonment issues. But then, didn't all the Donnelly kids?

"Not bad coaching, old man," Jack said when Josh and Hope reached them. "Bring back memories?"

"Who are you calling *old man*? I seem to remember

us playing on the same team, me showing you rookies the ropes."

"More like a senior lording over us underclassmen," Jack said.

"That I can see," Tessa said. "You do like to take charge."

Josh tensed, taking Tessa's words as a dig for missing their pre-practice meeting. He relaxed. Tessa teased. She didn't criticize. "Hey, my senior year when I was captain, I took us to a sectional championship. Jack was one of my minions. You were, what, in eighth grade?"

"Ninth," he said. "The only first-string freshman."

"I groomed him to take my position."

Tessa rolled her eyes.

"Right. You, coach and a lot of hard work on my part," Jack said. "We took the sectional championship the year after you graduated, too."

"Josh, excuse me," Hope interrupted. "Becca's here."

He looked over his shoulder to see Becca and his father walking toward them. He didn't want to know why he was here. If it was to see Hope practice, he'd missed it, as he missed most of Josh's games, except one. His mind shut down. He wasn't about to replay the embarrassment of that game. Josh waved at Becca and pointed to Hope. His sister-in-law and father stopped and he released the breath he'd unconsciously been holding.

"Grab your stuff and go meet Becca so she doesn't have to walk all the way out here. Let me know if you need a ride to practice on Wednesday."

"Sure thing, Josh." She raced across the grass.

"Bye, Hope," the boy with the soccer ball shouted.

Hope waved her hand behind her.

The boy trotted over to Josh. "Remember me?" he asked.

"Owen, from Hope's class."

"Yep. My brother and I are staying with the Hills now until our mother gets better."

Josh's gaze fixed on the fading bruise that covered the whole right side of Owen's face. Refocusing, his eyes locked with Tessa's, the compassion in them making him wonder how much the bruise had to do with Child Protective Services placing the boys with Jack and Suzi.

"Did you talk to my Scout leader about the Pinewood Derby?" Owen asked. "We're supposed to order the kits pretty soon."

"Sorry, pal, I was busy with work." He shifted his weight back and forth on his feet. He wasn't cut out for kid stuff. Everything was so important to them. It was too easy to disappoint them. In that way, he'd admit he was like his father.

"I told you I'd help," Jack said, throwing Josh a life-line.

"I'd still like you to, Coach Josh, if you can. You're more like my daddy." Owen's voice trailed off.

Lord, give me some direction. If he was like a convicted felon and his own father, he certainly didn't have it in him to be a role model for a young boy.

"My daddy has black hair like you and me."

A well-buried memory flickered in his mind. His dad's dark head bent over Jared's old bike, fixing it up and painting it to make the bike like new for Josh. At that moment, he'd wanted to be able to fix things, just like his dad. Josh's resistance crumbled. "Yes, I'll call Mr. Hazard. Tomorrow. Tessa, remind me in case I forget again."

"Will do." A smile played with the corners of her lips.

"We'd better get going," Jack said.

As he watched the guys leave, Josh attempted to recalculate the equation that was his life—the theater renovation, his family and his father's all-too-intrusive presence, coaching Hope's soccer team, helping Owen. Those factors all tied him to Paradox Lake when the final answer was supposed to be him getting a promotion and leaving. He closed his eyes and jiggered the pieces. They were all temporary situations, except for his father, and he had no good reason to stay for his father. He was good. He had everything under control.

"You're a good guy, Josh Donnelly." Tessa reached up and threw her arm around his shoulder.

The warmth that pulsed through him shot his neat and tidy recalculation to bits. He'd left Tessa and whatever weirdness he was experiencing about her out of the equation.

"You okay?" she asked.

"Yeah, fine. We need to collect and stow the equipment." He picked up the duffel bag she'd used to carry the equipment and uniforms and stuffed in the ball Owen had been kicking around.

Tessa touched his arm. "Hey, this is me." He gave her the same strangled look he'd given her when she'd flung her arm around his shoulder.

He grabbed her hand as she jerked away. She hadn't noticed the drop in temperature sunset had brought with it until his warm fingers closed around hers.

"Ignore me," he said. "Bad day."

If only she could. He dropped her hand and a chill ran through her at the loss of his warmth. She folded her open hoodie around her.

"One of the engineers gave me some rush modifications to do right at quitting time, so I didn't get to go home and change as I'd planned before I had to pick up

Hope. And we were late anyway." He closed the duffel and threw it over his shoulder. "I missed our strategy meeting completely. You had to run the whole practice."

"You can only control work so much." She knew as frustrated as he may have been, Josh wouldn't have hurried through the revisions. Nor would he have thought for a moment about saying he couldn't stay to do them.

"Then Dad showed up at the end of practice. You saw him?"

"Yeah, with Becca."

"Once he falls back into his old habits, the parents aren't going to want him at games, around the kids."

As futile as the effort might be, she had to try to soften his heart. "Maybe he won't. You could take things one day at a time with him like he's doing."

He rocked back on his heels, dismissing his father. "Then Owen threw me with the Pinewood Derby. I'd forgotten all about helping him with his car."

Tessa knew Josh didn't forget things, and he prided himself on keeping his word. The stress from his dad coming back was eating at him.

"Owen asked me that day I talked to Hope's class about my job. The expectation on his face today. I blew it." Josh fingered the duffel rope. "Did you walk over with all of this stuff? I didn't see your car."

She stepped in line with him, going with his subject change. "My grandmother dropped me off. Her car is in the shop, and she'd planned to go to the new Monday night Bible study at church. I figured I could catch a ride home with you."

"I'll consider it if you'll have a cup of coffee with me. I need to unwind."

"And coffee is going to help you unwind?"

"That and your company."

One corner of his mouth turned up in what she teased him was his killer smile, the smile she prided herself on being immune to. She straightened when she realized she'd leaned into his shoulder. Immune until right now.

"It's sad about Owen," she said, avoiding a direct answer to Josh's invitation.

"His mother did that?" Josh touched his cheek and repositioned his grip on the duffel bag, yanking it up on his shoulder.

"You don't know? Hope or the guys at the firehouse didn't tell you?"

"No, I haven't talked with them. I've been working overtime."

"The accident last week on Route 9—that was Owen's family."

A muscle twitched in Josh's jaw. "I saw the emergency squad carry him out. I didn't know it was him."

Tessa pressed her arm to her side to resist touching him again. Before tonight, she wouldn't have given it a thought.

"How is his mom? And Owen's brother? I heard the squad say there was another child in the car."

"Owen's little brother is fine, back at school like Owen. They were both in their booster seats. But Suzi told me their mother is still in critical condition. She's been in a coma since they airlifted her to Albany Medical Center, and her organs are shutting down. They don't expect her to live."

Josh blinked twice. "Another victim of alcohol. I'll keep her and the boys in my prayers."

"Her name is Gwen. Apparently, there's no family. The boys' father grew up in the foster system, and their mother's parents disowned her when she married their father."

"Who's in Dannemora? Owen told me." His expression hardened. "I don't understand how a parent can disown a child or a grandchild."

Tessa bit her tongue to avoid voicing her first thought: *The same way a child can disown or try to disown a parent.*

"I'm going to call Ted Hazard tonight and get the details about the Pinewood Derby." Josh arced the duffel bag into the bed of his truck and dug in his pocket for his keys.

Tessa pulled the passenger-side door as soon as she heard the lock click and settled in the cushy captain chair. The seat began warming as soon as Josh turned the ignition. He punched the truck into Reverse and circled back in a sharp curve.

Tessa squeezed the armrests. "I'd decided to take you up on that cup of coffee, but I might be safer walking in the dark."

"What?" He braked hard.

"Coffee. You wanted me to have a cup with you to wind down."

He blew out a breath and put the truck in Drive. "It fries me. Another family torn apart by a drunk. What's wrong with those people?"

Tessa cringed at the vehemence in the words *those people.* She was one of them.

She reached inside herself to forgive Josh his judgmental attitude. As far as she knew, he'd never even been a social drinker. He'd been strong enough to go against the crowd, stand up to anyone who called him out about having a Coke instead of a beer. While Josh would hotly deny the fact, in a roundabout way, his father was responsible for that strength—a strength that carried over to other parts of his life. His protective feelings toward his mother and Connor. His long recovery from the wounds he suffered in Afghanistan. His faith, even though he kept that more private.

"Sometimes it takes something big like an accident or the accumulation of a whole lot of small somethings, as with your dad, to stop drinking."

He slapped the steering wheel. "Dad. A good example of *What's wrong with those people*? He knew he drank too much, saw what it was doing to us and did it anyway. Mom, Pastor Joel, Gram and Harry tried to help him stop."

"Sobriety is something you have to want yourself, do for yourself. No one else can do it for you."

"What makes you such an expert?"

"I… I'm a…" *Tell him*, her inner self said, repeating what her sponsor had told her the last time they'd talked. *You're only as sick as your secrets*. But she didn't want to put more on Josh's plate with everything else he had. She *would* tell him. Just not now.

"No." He lifted his right hand from the steering wheel and flexed his wrist. "You already said it was something at college. I'm sure you don't want to talk about it any more than I want to talk about Dad or the drunk driver who hit Owen's mother's car. I've ranted enough for the night."

Tessa tugged at a loose thread on her hoodie sleeve. She didn't want to continue the conversation but knew she should. What kind of friend was she, to keep secrets? She glanced sideways at Josh's chiseled profile, and her heart thumped. A chicken friend who was afraid to be straight with him for fear of losing his friendship.

Josh pulled into a parking space on Main Street in front of the coffee shop.

She looked out the window as she pulled the door handle. "It's closed. I wonder why. They're usually open until nine."

"Probably the water main problem I heard about earlier today." He restarted the truck.

"We could have coffee at your place, watch a movie."

Josh circled around toward her grandmother's house and his apartment. "Never mind. I won't hold you to that coffee. Venting helped." He turned into her grandmother's driveway. "Thanks for listening."

"That's what friends are for."

She caught a glimpse of vulnerability in his eyes before he blinked and broke the warmth of his gaze. The chill of the night air made her shiver when she opened the truck door and slid out of the warm seat onto the driveway. The house sat dark behind the small porch light she'd insisted her grandmother leave on. "Oh, I forgot to tell you. I got the building permit today."

"Good, I'll get started after work tomorrow."

"Let me know if you need any help."

"I shouldn't. I've hired Myles. He's looking for extra work to buy a newer car. No cost to you. I'm paying him out of the money I'm saving on rent."

"Oh. I'll see you Wednesday at practice then. Five-fifteen?"

"I'll be there or text you if something comes up at work again."

Tessa dragged herself up the porch steps. Josh didn't want to hang out tonight. He didn't need her to work on the renovations. She fumbled in her pocket for her house key, digging it out from where it had fallen through a hole in the pocket and dropped between the sweatshirt and its Sherpa lining.

She had exactly what she wanted—Josh to be less a part of her life and her less a part of his. So where was the satisfaction of taking control and moving forward?

Chapter Seven

Tessa tossed a fourth shirt on her bed. Claire and Nick would be here in ten minutes to pick her up for the concert, and she still hadn't decided what to wear. Nick's cousin was going to meet them at the Sonrise Camp Auditorium, since he was driving from the opposite direction. She stared at the clothing. Her mind blanked. What was her date's name? Tessa pushed a damp curl from her forehead and addressed herself in the mirror, trying to get a grip.

"Sure, you haven't been on a date in a while, but you have been on dates before. No big deal. You were engaged once."

But that was before you were sober, and remember how it ended?

Her hands turned clammy. She shook them. "What does it matter if you and the guy don't hit it off, if Ben—" that was her date's name, Ben "—doesn't ask you out again? Nothing."

But Claire is so certain you're right for each other. You'd hate to disappoint her.

"Just get dressed. Claire is more likely to be mad at you if she and Nick show up and you're not even close to ready."

Tessa went back to her drawer and pulled out a soft, silky blouse in a jewel-toned cobalt. Josh had complimented her the two different occasions she'd worn it. Josh was a guy. Ben was a guy. She pulled the blouse on and smoothed it over her jeans. She and Ben would get along fine if he was anything like Josh. Well, anything like Josh was up until the past couple of weeks.

Tessa brushed her hair and started to pull it back before letting it drop around her shoulders. Josh seemed to like her hair down, or at least he commented on it when she wore it down. Having a guy pal could be handy for getting a male perspective. She placed the brush on the dresser. If she still had a guy pal. She hadn't seen or talked to Josh since Monday night's soccer practice, except for a couple of texts about the theater work. Rain had canceled Wednesday's practice. She'd walked over to the theater when the rain had stopped a couple of hours ago to make sure he and Myles had everything they needed for tonight's showing, half hoping Josh would be there working. He hadn't been.

Tessa smiled. Josh had posted whimsical "Pardon Our Appearance While We Change" signs with caterpillars crawling over the beginning words and butterflies sitting on and flying around the later words. While she was sure he'd lettered the signs and drawn the pictures, he had to have had help with the idea. Probably Hope. She picked up her blusher and applied it to her cheeks. Or maybe a new girlfriend had helped him and that was why she hadn't seen or heard from him this week. Tessa hugged her middle to get rid of the unsettled feeling she chalked up to predate jitters, not the thought that Josh had a new girlfriend.

Calming herself with the Serenity Prayer, she finished her makeup, stepped back and checked the overall picture.

Not bad, she told herself, boosting her determination to have a good time tonight.

"Tessa." A soft knock accompanied her name. "Your friends are here."

She opened the door. "I'm ready, Grandma."

"You look nice. Your hair is such a pretty combination of your mother's color and your father's curls. You should wear it down more."

"Thanks. Josh said that at Connor's wedding." Tessa spoke her earlier thought and tried to ignore the uneasiness that returned with the soft smile her words brought to her grandmother's face. It had been a friendly observation, like her reassuring him he looked handsome. As if he needed reassurance. Josh had enough ego for three people.

"Do you have a jacket?" her grandmother asked as they walked down the stairs. "The rain brought in a cold front."

Tessa glanced at Claire and Nick standing by the door. Neither of them had worn coats. "We'll be in the car, and the auditorium will be warm. I'm okay without."

"Hi, Tessa," Claire said. "This is Nick Brunner." The glow on her friend's face when she made the simple introduction warmed Tessa and left her empty at the same time.

Nick was exactly as Claire had described him, tall and muscular with Nordic blond hair and even features. He looked a lot like Tessa's former fiancé. And as they exchanged greetings, Tessa couldn't help hoping Nick's cousin had a different appearance—darker hair, a less bulky build and more chiseled features. She stilled, realizing she'd just described Josh.

"Have fun," her grandmother said as they left.

"We will," Tessa said, renewing her determination

to enjoy herself and her date and adding an addendum not to think about Josh.

On the drive to the auditorium, the three of them talked about Resurrection Light, a local Christian rock group that had made it nationally but always played home a couple times a year, usually as a charity benefit.

"You're going to love them," Claire said, "even more in person than their recordings I've played for you."

"I'm sure I will," Nick said in a voice that sounded more as if he'd like anything Claire said, liked or did than a comment on the group.

Nick's cell phone dinged, and he handed the phone to Claire. "Can you check my text? Probably Ben at the auditorium waiting for us impatiently."

Tessa glanced furtively at the dashboard clock. She hadn't delayed them. They were running right on time.

"Oh, no." Claire glanced over the seat back and Tessa's stomach sank.

"What?" Nick asked.

"Ben's not coming."

The sinkhole in her gut became a crater.

"Did he say why?" Nick asked.

"No, just 'sorry, can't make it.'"

Nick pulled into the auditorium lot and parked. "You guys go in. I'm going to call Ben." He handed them their tickets.

"Want me to pay you back?" Tessa asked.

"No, no skin off my back. Ben bought your ticket and his wasted one."

Claire touched his arm. "Not totally wasted. The proceeds are going to Jared Donnelly's motocross school for underprivileged kids and the Sonrise summer camp program."

"Still, the concert sold out early. Someone else could

have used the ticket." Nick punched a number into his phone.

"I'm so sorry, Tessa," Claire said as they walked to the building. "Ben's longtime girlfriend broke up with him a few weeks ago, and Nick thought it would be good for him to get out with other people. You were a good friend to agree."

"Hey, a free concert ticket, what's there not to agree about?"

"The blind date part. I seem to remember Josh and me having to do some convincing there."

Tessa remembered, too. Had Josh supported Claire because he'd thought she needed to get out with other people, hang with him less? She bit her lip. His support of Claire didn't mean he was ditching her. He was helping her goal of expanding her circle of close friends, even though he didn't know it.

They found their seats, and Nick joined them a couple of minutes later. "I should have known," he said. "His girlfriend called. She apologized. She wants to get back together. At least he didn't show up with her." Nick dropped into his seat. "Sorry, Tessa."

"It's okay, really."

Tessa leaned back in her seat, her earlier tension gone. She settled in to enjoy the concert, without her date and without thinking about Josh. As the warm-up singers finished their set, she felt a tap on her shoulder.

"Anyone sitting here?"

The surprise on Tessa's face was exactly what Josh had expected. He would have taken a picture to show her later if the flash on his phone wouldn't have disturbed the other concertgoers.

"Josh! What are you doing here?"

"I heard you were short a date." He bit the side of his mouth while she glanced from Claire to Nick and back to Claire.

"Don't look at me," Claire said. "Did you see me call or text anyone?"

Tessa shook her head, her chestnut curls swaying. He really liked when she wore her hair down.

"I ran into Josh on the way in," Nick said.

"You know each other?" Tessa asked.

"From the gym," Josh said. "Nick told me about your problem."

Tessa sat straight in her seat. "What problem?"

"This empty seat." He slid in beside her.

"But how did you get in?"

Josh could almost see her mind working.

"I know how much you like Resurrection Light. You didn't." Her face lit with amused suspicion.

"Didn't what?" He was enjoying busting on Tessa almost as much as he expected to enjoy hearing the band play.

"Show up at the auditorium door and wait to see if anyone had an extra ticket."

"You think I don't have anything better to do on a Friday night?"

"Well, I…"

"The truth is, I didn't have anything better to do tonight, nor did I show up without a ticket. Autumn was called for a home birth late this afternoon and there were complications. So Jon had to go meet her and the mother at the birthing center in Ticonderoga. He dropped off their tickets with Connor on his way. Connor called me and here I am."

Her exaggerated smile of exasperation relieved him of the niggling doubt that she might not want him crashing her evening. This was Tessa. Why would he even think that?

"Wait," Tessa said so loudly, the three rows in front and back of them had no trouble hearing her. "If you're here, who's handling the concession stand at the Majestic?"

"Not to worry. Myles's friend Kaitlyn was available."

"But, but I don't know her. She's handling the evening's money."

"I talked with Jack. He vouched for her, and you said she's good with math."

Tessa released a big sigh. "What am I going to do with you?"

Be my best friend, Josh thought, hating the neediness he felt.

Drew Stacey, the director of the Sonrise Camp and Conference Center stepped on stage to introduce Resurrection Light.

"They're going to start. You'd better get back to your seat, Josh," Claire said.

Tessa's eyes narrowed as she glanced over at Claire. He studied the soft line of Tessa's jaw and graceful curve of her neck. So she didn't want him to run off to his seat with Connor and Natalie, even though he'd pushed her into agreeing to the blind date, and then she'd been stood up.

"Natalie told me Connor got you guys almost front row seats. Tessa, it's okay with us if you want to go with Josh and take the other seat with Connor and Natalie."

"No can do, unless Tessa wants to sit on my knee."

"I do not."

Josh laughed at her indignation, but he'd expected no less. "Connor gave the other ticket away. To our father."

"Yeah," Nick said. "I love my dad, but given the

choice between a concert with him or a concert with friends, gotta say I'd go with the friends."

More so, if Nick had Jerry Donnelly as a father. Josh watched Claire study her hands in her lap. She'd gone to school with him and knew his father. Nick was from Crown Point. He didn't. Or at least not yet, until Dad did something stupid that showed up in the *Times of Ti*. Josh tensed when Claire leaned toward Nick as if she were about to say something. Something about his father?

"I know what you mean, Nick," Tessa said.

Claire leaned back and Josh relaxed, grateful for Tessa's redirection of the conversation away from his father.

"When I was in college, my parents paid me a surprise visit one weekend when they were in the States on a fund-raising tour. They have a mission church in Lesotho, Africa," she said for Nick's benefit. They offered to take me and some friends I was meeting out to dinner. We'd made plans to go to a local—"

Tessa's lips pressed together as if to say a word beginning with a b or a p and he mentally filled in the word *bar*. Had she hesitated to admit she'd been to a bar because of him and his possible reaction? She should know him better than that. He didn't drink, but he didn't condemn people who did responsibly.

Tessa's lips opened "College hangout to hear a group we all liked. I went to dinner with Mom and Dad but didn't blame my friends for sticking with our original plans."

Meaning he should sacrifice a good time for his father. He'd do that as soon as he saw dear old Dad do it first. And it didn't have to be for him. Josh pushed back more firmly in his seat and placed his arm next to Tessa's on the armrest. His plan to avoid contact with his father was proving harder than he'd thought it would be. He wished whatever weirdness was going on between him and Tessa would go away. Right now he needed his buddy who accepted him as he was, even when she disagreed with him.

Resurrection Light started their show and a minute later Josh and the rest of the audience were caught up in the group's music and message.

"That was their best concert yet," Tessa said, jumping up for a standing ovation when the group completed their last set.

Josh rose more slowly, noticing the loss of warmth along his arm and shoulder where Tessa had been pressed against him during the concert, as if a part of him had been pulled away. "Anyone want to go get something to eat?" he asked when the applause died down.

He wasn't ready to go home to his empty apartment, nor did he want to go back to the parsonage with Connor and Natalie to try out the pie she'd baked, as had been his plan before he knew his father was part of the deal.

"Sounds good to me," Nick said.

"The Three Penny should be open," Claire said, mentioning a local family restaurant. "Meet you guys over there."

Josh sensed Tessa tense beside him. "Afraid to be alone with me?" he teased to relieve the uneasiness, hers and his. "Promise I'll be on my best behavior."

"This is why I don't take you out in public," she said, back to her usual self.

Had he imagined her unease? "Does that mean you'd rather go back to my place?"

"Go ahead," she said to Claire and Nick, shaking her head. "We'll meet you at the Three Penny. I'll review public behavior with Josh on the way over."

Nick looked confused, and Claire laughed. "See you in a few minutes."

The minute it took Josh to text Connor that he wasn't coming over to the parsonage was enough of a delay to put them more in the crush of the traffic leaving than Claire and Nick, which made the ten-minute drive closer to twenty minutes. The time passed in what Josh convinced himself was companionable silence.

"Two?" the hostess asked when they got inside the restaurant. "You'll have a short wait."

"We're with friends who should have a table."

"Do you see them?" Tessa asked, rising on her tip-toes.

"In the back," he said.

The hostess waved them on and greeted the next group.

"Everyone at the concert must have had the same idea as us," Tessa said as they walked to the booth where their friends sat.

"That and the usual Friday nighters." He lifted his chin toward the people sitting at the bar.

Tessa's foot caught a chair leg and she tripped. He grabbed her elbow so she didn't fall. Her gasp of pain brushed against his ear, and he slid his arm down around her waist.

"You okay?" His gaze dropped to her open-toed shoes. "Do you think you broke your toe?"

"No, no. I'm fine."

He loosened his hold, expecting her to pull away. Instead, she moved closer, and he rested his hand back on her hip, directing her away from the bar.

When they got to the booth, a waitress was delivering Nick's and Claire's drinks. Tessa and Josh slid into the empty side of the booth. The waitress placed an ice tea in front of Claire and an open bottle of beer in front of Nick.

"It's Paradox Brewery's Classic Stout," Nick said as the waitress poured the beer in the glass in front of him. "I recommend it."

Tessa's mouth twitched as the dark liquid filled the glass.

The waitress pulled out her pad. "We have a couple other local beers on tap," she said, drawing Josh's attention from Tessa.

"No, thanks," he said. "I'm good with coffee." He waited for Tessa to comment on his caffeine "dependence."

She sat quiet, staring at Nick's beer.

"And you?" the waitress asked.

"I…" Her voice squeaked and she cleared her throat. "I'll take an ice tea."

Josh glanced at Nick and Claire. Neither of them appeared to think Tessa was acting or sounding odd. He must be imagining her fixation with Nick's drink. His father's return had his brain so muddled he could hardly think straight about anything. Josh clenched a fist under the table. He would not let his father dominate his life again, have him walking on eggshells and waiting for the other shoe to drop.

Josh was lounging against his truck in the school parking lot with his arms crossed in front of him when Tessa arrived for their Saturday pregame strategy session.

Early. That was more like her Josh. Her *friend* Josh, she corrected herself. "You here alone, mister?" she asked as she walked to the trunk of her car, where the equipment was.

He looked to his left and to his right, making her smile. "It appears I am."

"Want to give a girl a hand?" Tessa asked, batting her eyelashes before lifting the trunk door.

He pushed off and sauntered over. "Sure thing, pretty lady."

Tessa made a gagging sound. "Okay, enough. My fault. I shouldn't have started it."

Josh stepped beside her with a soft look in his blue eyes that disappeared before she could be certain it had really been there. She reached for the first thing she saw, the duffel bag.

"I'll get that," he said, gently brushing aside her hand.

His touch flowed over her, leaving a warm feeling in the pit of her stomach. He lifted the bag out, and Tessa gathered the orange cones into a stack, taking her time to give herself a moment before she faced him.

She closed the trunk and admired the smooth ease with which he threw the heavy duffel over his shoulder. "So with only our one practice to go on, what's your take on strategy?"

"After carefully analyzing the data I had, we should concentrate on keeping the right number of players on the field and make sure the kids move the ball toward our goal so they don't score for our opponents."

Tessa laughed. "Works for me."

Before they could start toward the field, Jack Hill pulled the Hill's Garage tow truck into the parking lot with Owen in the passenger seat. The little boy had his car seat belt off and the truck door open before Jack could walk around the front. Tessa held her breath as Owen jumped down onto the hard pavement.

"Hi, Coach Josh." Owen ran over. "Did you talk to Mr. Hazard about the Pinewood Derby?"

"Owen," Jack said. "Give me a minute to talk with the coaches, like I said on the way over."

"Okay."

"I have to drop Owen off early. I got a call for a tow job."

"No problem," Josh said.

Tessa let him answer for both of them out of a fear she'd laugh at Owen if she didn't keep her lips pressed together. The little boy hopped from one foot to the other in front of them as if he might explode with energy any moment.

"Thanks," Jack said. "Suzi will be over with Dylan in time to watch the game. She has to drive Kaitlyn to her part-time job first."

"Like I said. We're good," Josh said. "Owen can help us set up."

"You do what the coaches say," Jack told Owen, who gave him a wide-eyed nod.

Tessa's heart ached for the little boy. From what Suzi had told her, Owen and his mother and brother had moved to the area over the Christmas school break, so he'd had to adapt to a new school and kids mid-school year. And then there was the accident.

"You can help me set up the field," Tessa said.

Owen grinned and trotted beside her and Josh to the field. "I can take the cones apart for you. I'm real good at helping. I got the student of the week award at school last week for doing extra stuff for my teacher."

"And if you finish helping Coach Tessa before the others get here, I'll show you a few passing tips," Josh said. Josh pulled a ball from the duffel and tossed it in the air, knocking it forward with his head and racing over to where it landed as if he was the receiver. He dribbled it back to Tessa and Owen.

"Show-off," Tessa said before glancing at Owen. The smile had left his face. Had her teasing Josh upset him? Or did Owen think she was reprimanding him for bragging about his school award, although she didn't think what he said was a brag?

The boy scuffed the toe of his cleat against the grass. "I was hoping I could play goalkeeper," he said in a soft voice. "That's what I played last year on my other team."

"Sure, for part of the game, at least." Josh handed Owen two cones. "Run these down to the other end of the field. Do you remember how we had them at practice?"

"Yep, and thanks for letting me play keeper. I won't let the team down." Owen raced away.

"Do we have someone else who wants to play keeper?" Tessa asked. "I couldn't seem to interest anyone at practice and had to assign someone for my scrimmage team."

"I did, too, but that was before Hope missed the tying goal. After practice, she texted me asking to play keeper."

"What did you tell her?" Tessa twisted the Fitbit on her wrist. Josh liked to think of himself as the fun brother and pretty much did anything Hope asked of him. Maybe she should slip in something about being careful not to play favorites.

"I told her she could give it a try. I didn't say she could be in for the whole game or anything. I say we start with Hope because she asked first—and I'll tell Owen that—then we can switch at the half."

"Perfect."

"And don't worry, if Owen is the better keeper, I'll

have no problem if we put Hope in for less time in future games, if she even wants to continue in the position."

She should have known that as much as Josh loved his little sister, he wouldn't play favorites.

"What can I do next?" Owen asked, coming to a screeching halt in front of them.

"We need to place the rest of the cones," Tessa said, noticing some figures crossing the schoolyard toward the soccer field.

"Can you handle it without Owen?" Josh asked. "I need to talk with him for a minute. Guy stuff." He winked at Tessa over the little boy's head.

"I can do that." She lingered long enough to watch Josh crouch to Owen's level and say, "I talked with the scoutmaster, and we're all set to build that race car."

She hummed to herself as she put out the rest of the cones. Josh had told her more than once that he wasn't father material, that he had no frame of reference. Something else they had in common. Her parents had provided for her financially, and she knew they loved her, but neither had taken any real interest in her as a person. The mission church was their "baby." Tessa was fairly certain Josh's aversion to parenthood was one of the reasons his romantic relationships tended to be short. He laid out his expectations and limitations. Not that everyone took him at face value. When Josh was dating Lexi, he'd complained often enough that Lexi said she wasn't into kids at all and then made a show of cooing over and asking to hold any baby they encountered.

Tessa glanced over her shoulder at Josh and Owen before approaching a group of parents and kids who were walking to the field. Josh's hand rested lightly on Owen's shoulder while the boy explained something to him that needed a multitude of gestures. A pinprick of pain pierced her. Josh had no idea how much he had to offer a kid. It would be sad if he never had any of his own. She suspected he'd be the father he'd wished his father had been.

"Coach Tessa," Hope called, pulling Tessa from her thoughts. "Am I the first one here?"

"Nope, Owen's here, too."

Hope made a face, and Tessa hoped she wouldn't give Josh a hard time about sharing the goalkeeper position.

"Go ahead and check in with Josh. He has the roster."

Hope raced down the sidelines to her brother, while Tessa walked with Josh's brothers and their families. Becca and Natalie fell into step with Tessa as the guys and kids moved ahead of them.

"Your father-in-law isn't coming today?" Tessa asked.

"No, he has a meeting he wanted to go to," Natalie said.

Good, Tessa thought. She and Josh needed a day without the elephant in the room looming. Tessa just hoped Josh's father wasn't losing interest in his family as Josh had prophesized he would.

"The Donnelly cheering section all present and reporting for duty," Connor said when they reached Josh, Owen and Hope. "Where do you want us?"

On the word *all*, Josh shot a furtive glance past his family, probably making sure his father wasn't following.

"Front and center is good. We have Hope as first-half keeper. I just finished telling her we're going to switch her out for Owen the second half. He said he played keeper on a team last year."

Jared and Becca nodded their approval before joining the rest of the family in the second row of the bleachers.

The first half of the game ended with the Hazardtown Hornets behind one to zero and Hope more than ready to hand the face mask and pads over to Owen.

"So, where am I playing now?" Hope asked.

"We're going to let you rest for a few minutes," Tessa said.

The little girl checked Tessa's words with a frown at Josh.

"Yep," he said. "We talked about this. The team has two extra players, and Tessa and I want to give everyone equal playing time."

Hope huffed over to the players' area on the front bleacher. "That means I'll get like two minutes to play, and I didn't like being keeper."

Tessa saw Jared bend over to talk with Hope before the referee blew the whistle for the players to take their positions for the second half.

"Owen really knows his stuff," Josh said as the boy deflected yet another kick near the end of the game that looked like a sure goal for their opponents.

"Yes, he does. I wish we could get a goal, though."

As if hearing her wish, a Hornet's player caught a pass from Hope's friend Sophia and charged to the goal and scored. The parents and other spectators behind Tessa and Josh roared.

Josh called the player in. "Great job. Since the game is almost over, I'm going to have you sit out the last few minutes." He tilted his head toward the bleachers and Hope.

"Hope." Tessa motioned the girl to her. "Go in as right forward."

She raced in, and play restarted with Hope intercepting an opponent's pass almost immediately. Hope moved the ball through the other team's players until she had an open shot to Sophia near the goal.

"Pass!" Tessa shouted.

"Pass," Josh echoed, frowning when she didn't.

They both groaned when she kicked from too far out for the other team's keeper not to be ready to block the ball, which was headed in a trajectory that looked to be to the left of the goalpost anyway.

In readiness, the keeper positioned himself slightly left of the net to catch the ball, but it curved and hit the inside of the post bouncing across the line and into the net.

"She did it. Unbelievable." Josh slapped Tessa on the back so hard Tessa took a step forward.

"You okay?" he asked. "I didn't mean to…"

"I'm fine."

The referee whistled the end of the game.

"We won!" the kids screamed as they circled around her and Josh, jumping up and down as if they'd aced a championship game rather than winning the first game of the season.

Yeah. She was fine. Better than fine. Josh had slapped her on the back as if she was one of the guys. His touch hadn't evoked any unsettled feelings. She didn't see any guarded emotion in his eyes. Maybe things between them were getting back to their old comfortable friendship.

Chapter Eight

"Hi. I've been stood up."

"What?" Tessa said into her cell phone. Josh had had a date at seven-thirty in the morning on a Wednesday? She took a gulp of coffee to clear her mind. She shouldn't have stayed up so late finishing that suspense novel. But if she hadn't finished, she might not have gotten any sleep at all.

"I'm at the Majestic. We were going to remove the seats in the area where you want to put the tables. But Myles is a no-show. There was some problem with the science rooms at the community college yesterday, and his lab was rescheduled to this morning."

"Wait. Shouldn't you be at work?" She knew Josh was hoarding his vacation time at GreenSpaces so that he could take off to move when the project manager promotion he wanted came along.

The phone crackled and went silent for so long, Tessa thought she'd lost service. She checked the left corner of her phone. No, she had four out of five dots.

"You there?" she asked.

"Yeah. Connor told me our father is coming in to

GreenSpaces today to do an estimate for painting the interior walls. I thought it best if I wasn't there."

"What if he gets the job? Do you have enough vacation time to take off however many days the painting takes?" She hated the strident note in her voice, but Josh's hiding from his father was getting on her nerves.

"He'll be working evenings. I'll come in early, rather than work late. It'll give me more time to work on the theater. Speaking of which, are you free to come over and help me today?"

She wanted to say she'd love to as long as his father wasn't there in spirit, coming between them. "Let me finish my coffee. Need me to bring anything?"

"Just yourself."

Tessa didn't even attempt to figure out why Josh's statement made her pulse quicken. She didn't want anything today to alter the friend status she felt she'd regained Saturday.

"I'll buy you lunch," Josh said.

"You don't have to do that. I already said I'm coming."

"Lunch is a lot cheaper than what I'd be paying Myles for the morning."

"So, you only need my help this morning?" She wanted the work done as soon as possible and didn't mind spending the whole day.

"Whatever you want. Myles and I'll be working through the afternoon."

"Okay. See you in about fifteen." Tessa finished her coffee and entertained a fleeting thought about running upstairs to put on makeup. She shook her head. All she was doing was going over to help Josh with the theater construction.

"Hey," she called after she pushed open the interior theater door. "Assistant Hamilton reporting for duty."

Josh rose from the squat position he'd been in to look under the front row seats. "Come on down and I'll show you what we're doing." He picked up a paper from one of the seats.

She walked down the right-side aisle and grasped the edge of the architect's plans closest to her to get a better view.

He dropped his hold on that side of the plans and pointed at the front seating diagram, a faint hint of his woodsy cologne or, more likely, soap, teasing her nose.

"According to the plans, you want to come back at least thirty feet for tables. With the aisle-buffer between the dinner-theater area and the regular movie seating, we need to remove five rows of chairs."

Tessa looked back at the seating rows and swallowed. "That many?" She wanted the dinner theater conversion to add to her revenues, not limit her regular weekend movie income.

He flipped another smaller paper on top of the plans and she leaned in for a closer look.

"Your twelve-month spreadsheet of average theater attendance shows that even your top five showing nights for the period, adjusted up five percent, would fill only a few seats more than seventy-five percent of the post-renovation theater seating."

The numbers blurred. Was this all a crazy pipe dream? Should she call a halt to it before Josh invested his time and she invested Jared's money and her remaining money from her grandfather? Her lip trembled and she sensed Josh's gaze on her. She turned from the spreadsheet toward him and he lowered his head closer to the sheet, closer to her. She parted her lips and a soft but intense look burned in his eyes. Did he feel that bad for her? Was he going to kiss her to make it better? That would be in character for Josh.

Except it wouldn't make anything better. It would change their relationship too much—at least on her part. Ruin the comfortable friendship she wanted back. Only she couldn't lie to herself that she didn't want him to kiss her. Just this once to get it out of her system. It wouldn't mean anything. She closed her eyes and waited.

He brushed her cheek with his forefinger so softly she wasn't sure she hadn't imagined it. "I meant that as a good thing."

She blinked her eyes open.

"You have seating capacity for increased movie patronage spillover from dinner theater patrons," he said.

"Yeah, right. I lost my confidence for a minute." Disappointment slowed her heartbeat to normal. "I've planned this, prayed on it. I know it'll work."

"It sure will, as long as we get the work done by the start of tourist season."

"So let's get going. What do you need me to do?" She folded the plans and spreadsheet over into Josh's hands.

He carried them to the near wall where he had his tools and came back holding a power drill like a gun and revving the motor.

Tessa held her hands up in surrender, glad for his comic relief. "I didn't do it, Sheriff. I didn't do it."

"I know, but you're going to." Josh made a diabolical face and revved the tool again. "Over to the wall, woman." He squatted in front of the first seat by the wall and motioned her to join him. "I need you to remove the bolts from the seats and I'll carry them out the side door and put them in the truck to be carted away."

Tessa assessed the five rows of seats. "How many do you think will fit?"

Confusion spread across his face, followed by the glint of understanding. "Not my truck. I made a deal with Your Trash, Someone's Treasure to haul away the seats and sell them on consignment. The box truck is in the alley by the door."

"Your Trash, Someone's Treasure?"

"It's a new business. Reputable. I checked. Don't worry, the sales proceeds will come to you."

"Sounds good, but I wish you'd cleared it with me beforehand." On the one hand, she appreciated Josh's initiative. He had a way of turning anything and everything into money. But the theater was her business.

He revved the tool again. "I was going to this morning. It was spur of the moment. GreenSpaces hired him to clear out an old warehouse Anne recently bought as-is. The owner was waiting to see my boss and I got to talking with him. It's the perfect solution. Better than trashing the seats."

"True." Tessa joined him on the floor. "So, how do I do this?"

Josh showed her the bolts and how the ratchet bit fit on them, and they got to work. After removing the bolts from the last seat in the last row, Tessa surveyed the cleared floor space visualizing a flat floor space filled with multicolored bistro tables and chairs. She heard Josh come in through the side door and turned, excitement bubbling. "I...we're really going to do it."

"You had a doubt?"

She grabbed his hand and squeezed it. "How could I with you behind me?"

"Exactly."

Tessa brushed her hands on the sides of her denim

capris. "I'm starved. Let's get cleaned up for lunch. Where are we going?"

"We could walk to the pizza-sub shop."

"Works for me." She started up the aisle to the lobby and restrooms to clean up.

Josh stepped in line with her. "Food reminds me. Are you going to the singles group's barbecue tomorrow evening?"

"No, a friend is going to be in Elizabethtown and I'm getting together with her."

Tessa pushed open the ladies' room door and walked in. She stood in the dark for a moment. The friend was her sponsor, and the plans were dinner, a tour of Maura's home since she hadn't gone to the open house and a discussion of how to tell Josh. Tessa turned on the light and the sink faucets. She shouldn't put off telling him any longer but wanted to talk with Maura to get her words right so she wouldn't totally alienate him. Tessa ripped a towel from the dispenser. If that was even a possibility. She tossed the towel in the trash and pushed tomorrow and telling Josh from her head, not wanting to ruin the time she had with him today.

Josh was waiting for her in the lobby. "It'll be shorter if we go out the side door and down the alley," he said. "I have the key you gave me, if you don't have yours with you."

As they approached the side door, it cracked open. Josh stepped in front of her, not that she sensed any danger. This was the middle of the day in Schroon Lake. Her breath caught when his father stuck his head in and peered around.

"What are you doing here?" Josh demanded.

"Looking for Tessa," his father answered in a conversational tone. "Betty, her grandmother, hired me to do some painting and house maintenance. She suggested I stop by here and see if you need any painting done on the theater. The front door was locked, so I tried this one."

"No," Josh said before she could open her mouth. "We have everything here covered."

"Excuse me. Your father was talking to me."

Josh pushed by them. "I'll wait for you outside."

"Sorry about that," Jerry said.

"I understand. You and Josh…"

"I suppose you do," Jerry said.

Tessa tensed with the unsettling notion that he knew her secret. But he couldn't. Grandma wouldn't have told him. She shook off the thought, even more determined to come clean with Josh as soon as she talked with Maura.

"Josh was right, though," Tessa said, seeing Josh's stubborn jaw and sharp cheekbones reflected in his father's face. "I don't need any painting done. If you want, you can go out the front door. It'll lock behind you."

"I probably should. I've riled Josh enough. Your grandmother didn't say he was here."

"Give him time to come around," she said, hoping that was true. She waited until she heard the front door open and click closed before joining Josh.

"I can't take it," he said when she stepped into the bright noon sun. "He turns up everywhere I go."

She placed her hand on his forearm. He jerked as if he was going to shake her hand off, but stopped before he did and placed his hand over hers. The ping-pong game in her gut slowed.

"I've got to do something to get through until GreenSpaces hands me my ticket out of here. Maybe

Al-Anon like you said before. Learn the rules of his game so he doesn't keep ambushing me."

That wasn't even close to the reason she'd recommended Al-Anon, but that didn't matter if it got him to attend meetings. She allowed herself the hope he'd come to accept his father in his life and her admission—if not right away, later.

Josh walked up the garage stairs to his apartment. His new earlier work schedule hadn't seemed like such a great idea this morning when he'd dragged himself out at six-thirty, but getting home before five in the afternoon was all right. He'd have time to unwind before heading over to the Hazards' boat landing on Paradox Lake for the singles group's barbecue. He wished Tessa was going. He might need his wing woman to deflect Lexi's never-subtle hints.

He and Lexi had had some fun times together, but anything between them had been over for months. Why couldn't she just be his friend now, like Tessa? But none of the women he'd dated ever became plain friends after they'd parted. He put his key in the apartment door and paused. Good thing for him, he and Tessa had never dated. Even better that he hadn't given in to the insane urge he'd had in the theater yesterday to kiss her. Becoming romantically involved was the only thing he could think of that could ruin their friendship.

Despite it still being spring, hot humid air slapped Josh in the face when he opened the door. He walked across the room to the window AC unit and turned the dial to On. He needed to check with Tessa and her grandmother about him putting in a new window unit with a programmable thermostat. He could justify his cost by the electricity he could save over the summer, not to mention his comfort. Above the hum of the AC turning on, he heard a strange scraping sound coming from the back of the garage. He walked to the window, picturing the trees behind the building. None were close enough to scrape it, and there was no wind to speak of.

The scraping grew louder as he neared the window. Looking out he couldn't see anything to either side of the AC unit. Josh went back downstairs to see what was going on. As he rounded the back corner of the garage, he nearly walked into an older, but well-kept, black pickup truck. Past the vehicle, he spotted a man on a ladder, scraping the old paint off the garage wall below the AC unit. He grimaced. His father.

"Josh." His father started down the ladder at a pace far slower than he'd expect from a man in his midfifties.

Josh stiffened, his heart thumping in fear and his stomach roiling with disgust as he waited for his father to miss a rung and stumble and fall.

"I expected to be finished and gone before you got home," his father said. "Betty said you usually work late."

"My schedule's changed. I get home by five now."

Josh watched his father close the space between them in a perfectly straight line. As his father reached around for a mini-vac in the back of the truck, Josh braced himself for the all-too-familiar stink of booze to hit him. When it didn't, the force of his tension dissipating drained him.

His father lifted the vacuum. "I'll clean up and be out of your way. I've got a meeting to get to tonight."

Josh stood tall. Was that supposed to mean something to him? "Take your time." He turned to go back inside.

"See you Sunday at Edna and Harry's," his father called back at him.

Harry's eighty-fifth birthday party. There was no way he could skip that.

"Yeah, Sunday." He kicked a stone out of his way. Maybe he could get Tessa to come with him. He was sure his grandmother would have invited her grandmother, and his brothers would have their wives with them. He'd text Tessa when he got inside.

Josh bounded up the apartment stairs and remembered Tessa was doing something with a friend tonight. He'd wait until tomorrow. But he had to do something to get a grip on his life, control his father's influence on it— since the old man showed up everywhere Josh turned.

A paper blew off his desk as he passed it on his way to the bedroom to change into jeans and a T-shirt for the barbecue. The list of Al-Anon meetings that he'd printed out last night. He skimmed it. There was one in Elizabethtown tonight at seven.

Might as well check it out. He didn't really want to go to the barbecue without Tessa, and what did he have to lose? The details said it was a step meeting. Steps sounded logical to him. Steps to guide him back into control.

An hour and a half later Josh stood at the door of the meeting room in the Old Stone Church in Elizabethtown. He glanced through the window. The room was set up with chairs in rows, as he'd hoped, rather than around a table, and he didn't see anyone he knew right off. He rolled his shoulders. Good. He could keep his distance. He twisted the doorknob, slipped inside and slid into a chair in the corner a couple of rows from the back. While the clock up front clicked off the five minutes until seven, Josh heard the door open and shut a few more times and people take seats behind him.

Finally, a man stepped up in front and introduced

himself as Roger. "Welcome everyone, especially if you're joining us for the first time."

Josh squirmed as Roger panned the room, starting with him.

"We hope you'll find in this fellowship the help and friendship we've been privileged to enjoy. We urge you to try our program. It has helped many of us find solutions that lead to serenity. So much depends on our own attitudes, and as we learn to place our problem in its true perspective, we find it loses its power to dominate our thoughts and our lives."

That sounded good to Josh.

"We're a step group. We focus our meetings on the Twelve Steps, one of Al-Anon's three Legacies, along with Al-Anon's Twelve Traditions and Twelve Concepts of Service. We start our meeting with our group motto." He pointed at a whiteboard on the wall behind him.

Most of the room joined in saying, "I didn't cause it. I can't cure it. And I can't control it."

"Let's do that again with the new people," Roger said.

"I didn't cause it. I can't cure it," Josh said in a low voice, stumbling on the last, "and I can't control it." That was why he'd come, for control. He pushed forward in his seat, ready to stand and leave when a voice in his head said *give it a chance*, echoing his earlier thought. *What do you have to lose?* He slid back and prayed. *Lord, if that was You, show me a reason to stay.*

"Tonight we're discussing the second step, coming to believe that a power greater than ourselves can restore us to sanity."

Josh had his reason to stay. He understood God having a plan for him, leading him to sanity. If He wanted him to stay, Josh would.

"Who wants to share?" Roger asked. "Al-Anon is an anonymous fellowship. Everything said here, in the group meeting and member-to-member, must be held in confidence. Only in this way can we feel free to say what's on our minds and in our hearts and help one another."

Even with anonymity, Josh couldn't imagine sharing. He was here to learn from them, come to a few meetings to get the information he needed and be done.

A woman stood. "I'm Sandy."

"Hi, Sandy," the group said.

For the next hour, Josh listened to the others share and discuss the evening's step.

Roger stood in front again and said, "It's after eight. Anyone who wants more information or has questions can come up after our closing. We close with the Serenity Prayer." Again, he pointed at the whiteboard, and everyone stood.

When they'd finished the prayer, Josh wished he could say his heart was lighter, but it wasn't. He went to the table in front of the room to pick up some literature. Maybe he would understand everything better if he studied before coming to another meeting.

"Good to see you here." Another man standing by the table welcomed Josh and introduced himself.

"Josh. Have we met?" Josh tightened his grip on the flyer he held and checked his memory. Did he know this guy from a GreenSpaces job or his camp-flipping renovations? He'd hoped Elizabethtown was far enough from Paradox and Schroon Lake to avoid running into anyone he knew.

"I don't think so." The man shook his head. "Will we see you next week?"

"Sure." Josh loosened his hold on the flyer. If he came back. But he had to do something.

Avoiding eye contact with the people lingering in the hall, he managed to walk to the stairs leading down to the church lobby at a normal pace. He blinked. Tessa stood in the lobby, talking with another woman. He'd know her anywhere, even from the back. She must have been at the meeting, come in later and sat behind him.

She went to Al-Anon meetings. That's why she was so big on them and AA.

He looked again to make sure he wasn't wanting the woman to be Tessa so he'd have someone to explain things and come with him next time. He took the steps two at a time. Weird that she hadn't seen him sitting ahead of her in the meeting.

"Tessa," he said as he hit the floor.

She turned, eyes wide.

He drew back. She must not want people to know she went to Al-Anon. *Of course.* Otherwise, she would have invited him to come with her. But he wasn't *people.* He was her close friend or thought he was. Why had she told him she had plans with a friend? Maybe the meeting was the plans. She went to Al-Anon. So what? What was the big secret about that?

At the sound of Josh's voice, every ounce of air in Tessa's lungs whooshed out. She gasped to draw some back in.

"Are you okay?" Maura asked.

"No. Excuse me." She felt her sponsor's eyes on her as she forced one foot in front of the other until she and Josh had closed the space between them.

"Hey." Josh followed his greeting with a soft smile. "Didn't you see me in the meeting?"

"No," she answered in all honesty.

"I was over in the left corner, near the back. Since I didn't see you, I figured you came in after me and sat in the far back."

"Josh… I…" She took his hand and pulled him toward a small empty sitting room off the lobby. It had a wall of windows facing the lobby but would still give them some privacy to talk. His fingers closed around hers, the enveloping strength and warmth squeezing her heart until she couldn't bear the pain.

"What?" His forehead creased. "Are you okay?"

As okay as I can be. She gulped a breath and fixated on the cross hanging on the far wall of the room. *Dear Lord, stand with me. Guide me to say, do, what's best for Josh and his healing.*

She pulled her gaze from the cross. "Please sit."

He lowered himself into one of the overstuffed chairs while she crossed the room and looked out the window at the front lawn of the church.

"What's wrong? You're scaring me," he said when she didn't immediately turn back to face his question.

She turned and swallowed the lump in her throat. Not much scared Josh, at least, that he'd admit to. But he couldn't be half as scared as she was. His wide-eyed panic challenged that thought.

"Sit down and tell me. We're buds. I can take it, whatever you have to say." His normal bravado returned.

Tessa walked back and stood beside him, unable to look him in the eye. She rested her hand on the back of his chair. "I wasn't at your Al-Anon meeting. I was at another meeting." She dug her nails into the soft padding of the chair back. "An Alcoholics Anonymous meeting."

Josh looked over his shoulder at her, his eyes darkening with understanding.

"Yes," she said, fighting to keep the pain from her voice. "I'm a recovering alcoholic like your father. Five years sober." *As if that would make any difference to Josh.* Hadn't he said once a drunk, always a drunk?

Josh pushed himself from the chair so roughly, it flipped back onto the floor. "No," he shouted.

Several people in the lobby, including Maura and Josh's father, looked in the windowed wall.

Tessa touched Josh's arm, and he jerked it away. "I can't deal with this. You. I can't." He charged out of the room, brushing by Maura and the others in the lobby, glancing back at her through the glass before disappearing out the main lobby door.

Anger, hurt, she could take. But the look of pure disgust on his face cut her to the core in a way that might not ever heal. She crumpled in a chair, buried her face in her hands and wanted a drink with a fierceness she hadn't felt in years.

The sound of the door opening and closing made her lift her head. Maura walked over, righted the other chair and sat.

"That wasn't how I wanted him to find out," Tessa said.

"I know."

"I should have told Josh long ago, like you said."

"That time's gone. It's a new day. Focus on tonight," Maura said. "Do you still want to go for coffee with Pete and Jerry? I think you should."

Josh's father. He'd been at the meeting tonight, and when she pointed him out to Maura, her sponsor had suggested they include him and his sponsor, Pete, in their usual after-meeting coffee group.

Tessa looked out the window. "Where is Jerry? He didn't go after Josh, I hope." She shuddered at what that confrontation could do to both of the Donnellys.

"He did, but Pete stopped him. They went ahead to the diner."

Tessa bent and picked up her bag from the floor. "I'll go. I don't trust myself to go home."

"Do you want to pray?" Maura asked.

What she wanted was to crawl into a hole somewhere, preferably with a bottle of something. "I think I'd better." For the first time in a very long time, Tessa had doubts that it would help.

By the time Tessa pulled her car behind Maura's SUV in the diner parking lot, she felt marginally more in control. Maura waited at the door while she trudged her way across the parking lot.

"If you'd rather not go in," Maura said, "I can text Pete, and we can go back to my house instead."

"That would be the easy way out," Tessa said more to herself than her friend.

The corner of Maura's mouth quirked up. "The idea isn't to make things as hard for yourself as you can."

"But that's my usual approach." Tessa stepped by Maura and opened the door. "And getting to know his father better may be the only way I have to salvage my friendship with Josh."

"Keep in mind that friendship involves two people. If he can't accept you for who you are…"

Tessa lifted her hand. "I'm only too aware of that, and I don't know whether he can accept me or if I should even expect him to."

Maura shook her head, a signal that she wasn't going to join her pity party. "There's Jerry in the back booth."

Tessa's gut clenched when she saw Jerry motion to

them with a smile that was pure Josh. *Or Josh's smile was pure Jerry.*

"Where's Pete?" Maura asked as she slid into the booth seat after Tessa.

"He has an early day tomorrow. I assured him I was in good hands with you ladies."

Tessa swallowed the distaste of Josh's father flirting with them, everything she'd heard about his womanizing rushing through her head.

"Yeah," Maura said. "Pete mentioned he'd taken on a second job as a substitute morning school bus driver."

Tessa stared at Maura's non-reaction to Jerry's comment. He was old enough to be her father. Didn't she catch the inflection in his words? Jerry's phrasing was different, but his voice sounded exactly like Josh's did when he was talking up a woman.

"He told me they had more openings, but I don't have ten years of a clean license like he does. I just got mine back. Never had a license in California after my old New York one expired. The tip Pete gave me about the painting gig at GreenSpaces panned out, though."

Tessa set her jaw. *GreenSpaces, the garage apartment and the trim on Grandma's house. Everywhere you can be in Josh's face.*

"And—" he nodded to her "—Tessa's grandmother was kind enough to offer me more work," Jerry said, "on the flimsy reference that I used to mow her mother's lawn for her when I was a kid."

"Sounds like a good start establishing your business," Maura said.

The arrival of their waitress saved Tessa from having to add her encouragement. She admitted to herself she'd agree if Jerry wasn't the catalyst that had started the chain reaction that was causing her friendship with Josh—her life—to implode.

"What can I get you?" the waitress asked.

"Do you have chamomile tea?" Tessa asked.

"Sure do," the waitress answered.

"I'll take a cup."

Jerry glanced at Maura, who was reading a text on her phone. "Make mine coffee, black," he said.

Another way he was like Josh. She had to stop the comparisons before she fueled her tension into a killer headache.

"Nothing for me." Maura put away her phone, and the waitress left. "That text was from my husband. He got a call from work to come in and fix an equipment malfunction. I have to meet him on his way over there and retrieve the kidlets. That offer to stay at my house tonight is still open, Tessa."

She wavered. "I'm okay. I'd like to stay and talk with Jerry."

"Talk to you tomorrow," Maura said.

"Going to read me the riot act?" Jerry asked once Maura was out of hearing range.

Tessa rubbed her temples. "For what?"

"Being an alcoholic, being Josh's father, returning to the area—take your pick."

She took a packet of sugar from the sugar caddy while the waitress placed two mugs and a small stainless-steel teapot on the table, poured Jerry's coffee and left. How much of their conversation had the woman heard? She ripped the top off the packet. What did it matter? She didn't know the waitress.

Jerry watched her over the rim of his mug. His eyes, at least, were different from Josh's, more hazel than blue.

"No riot act. Just a question. Why did you come back

to Paradox Lake? I know, to make amends. But why stay? You must have been doing all right in California to be where you are with the program."

He lowered the mug to the table. "When I hit rock bottom, I realized that the only things I'd ever had of value in my life were here. I've lost Gail, Josh's mother, for good. She has someone else, and I'm truly happy for her. But the boys." His voice went gruff. "They mean the world to me."

"Me, too," she said.

He cocked his head.

"About hitting bottom and reaching for the best part of my life when I started to climb out, coming home to my grandmother and grandfather. When I was growing up, I spent a lot of time with them and my other grandmother in Batavia. She's gone now. My parents are missionaries in Africa," she said, as if that explained things.

"Your grandmother said you're close to Josh, too."

Tessa sipped her tea. "We're good friends, or we were good friends."

"He thought you were at the meeting with me?"

"No, he didn't know I'm an alcoholic."

"Oh." Jerry tapped his fingers on the table. "The other day at the theater, I assumed he did. I'd seen you at the Saranac meeting before we met."

"I should have told him. Maura's hammered me on that enough times."

"Was it because of me? I mean his opinion of me?"

She placed her mug on the table with a thud. "Everything isn't about you. But you scarred him bad, and he believes once a drunk, always a drunk—or so he's said repeatedly. He has no confidence in AA or any other recovery program."

"But you got him to go to an Al-Anon meeting. I

thank you for that. I hate to see him—any of my boys—in pain, especially because of me."

"No, I suggested he try a meeting. Connor and Jared probably have, too. Josh made his own decision to go." She half snorted, half huffed. "My surprise may have put him off going to any more."

"It's a start to his healing."

"Or a test of mine," she said under her breath.

"Pardon?"

"Maybe God is testing me. I want a drink tonight more than I have in years." She crossed her arms on the table and leaned toward Jerry. "My recovery has been relatively easy. I came to Grandma and Grandpa's from rehab. They were one hundred percent behind me. The first people I connected with were from the singles group at church. That's where I met Josh. Like Josh, the others don't drink, so they didn't think it odd that I don't. Josh, the theater and church and civic activities keep me busy. Maura is the perfect sponsor. I've had it easy."

"How long have you been sober?" Jerry asked.

"Going on five and a half years."

"Continuous?"

"Yes."

"And before that?"

"I wouldn't admit I had a problem. I thought I could control my drinking. How about you?"

"I got my one-year chip before I came back here. I had six months before that, before I relapsed a second time. We don't get do-overs, which in my case I don't deserve. The past is the past. But one thing the program has shown me is that we get start-overs."

Tessa sat back in the booth. "Can I ask you a favor?"

"Ask away."

"I know it's a little out of your way from the parsonage, but would you follow me home and see me into the house?" Her pulsed raced. "I want to make sure I don't make any stops on the way."

"Sure. You're the first real lady who's asked me to escort her home in a good long time." He winked at her.

"Hey, work the program, and I may not be the last."

As she drove the winding mountain roads home with Jerry's truck reassuringly behind her, Tessa mulled his words about starting over. Could her coming clean with Josh be a start-over for them, for their friendship? An opportunity for their relationship to become more? Her heart skipped a beat. All she had to do to find out was get him back on speaking terms with her.

Chapter Nine

Josh couldn't avoid Tessa forever. Nor did he really want to. But he was making a good show of it. Exhibiting far more cowardice than he'd felt during all his military service, he'd called Tessa at her grandmother's house number last night, Friday night, when he knew she'd be at the theater. He'd left a message with Mrs. Hamilton to tell Tessa he wouldn't be at the soccer game. Much to Hope's disappointment, he'd let himself be talked into working today. His sister had been quick to text him that they'd won anyway without him.

He pulled his truck into the parsonage driveway to pick up Connor for another Al-Anon meeting tonight. This one was men only. He'd told Connor coming with him was payback for all the times he'd protected him from Dad when he was a kid, but knew his baby brother would have come just for the asking. Josh honked the horn when Connor didn't come right out. He didn't want to risk running nine into their father, who was staying there, and being reminded that Dad and Tessa had been together at the AA meeting. Over the past two days, somehow her being friendly with his father had started bothering him more than the fact she'd *been* an alcoholic. She didn't fit the picture he had of a drunk, *recovering* or not. He'd never seen her take a drink, let alone drunk. More likely, she'd drunk too much in college like lots of people he knew and had blown that out of proportion.

"You in a hurry?" Connor asked as he climbed in the cab.

"Not so much as I didn't want to see Dad."

Josh could tell by his brother's expression that he was biting his tongue. But they'd discussed Dad as much as he wanted to when he'd stopped in Connor's office at the church after work yesterday.

"How are you doing?"

"Better since we talked yesterday. I read the Bible verses you suggested. But like I said, I thought Al-Anon would give me some control."

"You didn't cause it. You can't cure it. You can't control it."

"Smart aleck. So why am I going back?"

"I wasn't being flippant. You have feelings for Tessa and, no matter how much you deny it, for Dad, and they've both brought chaos into your life."

"That's the understatement of the year. I'm thinking more and more that it's time for me to take my life out of the chaos."

"Bingo. That's what Al-Anon is for. Reclaiming *your* life."

Josh slowed the truck for the turn into the mental health clinic in Ticonderoga. No chance of seeing Tessa or his father here. Tessa was working, and he'd checked to make sure there was no concurrent AA meeting. But that didn't stop him from scanning the lot for his father's truck. He should have done that Thursday.

"I was thinking more along the lines of taking my life

elsewhere," he said, ignoring the pang he felt. He was so messed up he didn't know if it was about leaving the Paradox Lake area or about subjecting himself to another meeting. "I heard there's going to be an opening for a drafter at the GreenSpaces main office in Boston." He turned off the truck and pulled his door handle to signal the end of conversation.

Connor wouldn't let him off that easy. "I thought the cost of living was too high there compared to the pay to take anything less than a project manager."

Josh sat, door half open, not wanting to take their conversation public in the parking lot. "I can cut my personal expenses, save less."

"So you can run away from Tessa and Dad, rather than face reality. You, my childhood hero, playing the coward?"

Josh got out of the truck and slammed the door. "I've said all I need."

"Hey, I was goading you, except for the you being my childhood hero part, bro, to get it all out." Connor sprinted to catch up to Josh. "Tessa is still Tessa. You still have your friendship or whatever it is the two of you have going on."

"I know. That's the problem." Josh stopped and pressed the key fob to lock his truck. "And, as far as I know, Dad is still Dad." He turned Connor's words against him, itching for an argument to fill his hollow insides, to give him an excuse to turn around and go home. Despite his National Guard training and all he'd seen in Afghanistan, he *was* a coward. He didn't want to face reality and work things out between him and Tessa. He wanted to go back to where they used to be.

Josh yanked open the clinic door. "After you."

He let Connor go in first and followed him to the

meeting room. Of course, *Pastor* Connor marched right down and took a seat at the front table. He sat next to him and stretched his legs out into the open space between the table and the wall.

"Hey, Connor." A guy their age Josh didn't know sat on the other side of his brother and began talking to him.

"Josh," Connor said when the guy paused, "this is Michael."

Michael reached down the table to shake hands. "Nice to meet you. You're new here?"

And Connor wasn't by the looks of things. "Yes, I am," Josh said.

A few more men arrived, not nearly as many as had been at the Elizabethtown meeting. Most greeted Connor by name. Before Josh had time to question his brother about that, a man who'd been there when they'd arrived started the meeting.

"Anyone else want to share?" the leader asked after most of the men had spoken. Connor raised his hand.

"I'm Connor," he said, although Josh strongly suspected they all knew that.

"Hi, Connor."

"I've been coming to this meeting off and on for a while. More on since my alcoholic father moved back to the area and in with me. I want to thank everyone for the support you've given me."

Connor glanced at Josh as he sat down. Was that some kind of cue? Was he supposed to jump up now? He stared at his feet. He wasn't Connor. The metal folding chair became harder and more uncomfortable as the remaining men shared. Finally, only he and Michael were left.

"Anyone else?" the leader asked.

Michael nodded. "Hi, I'm Michael."

"Hi, Michael."

Michael proceeded to give a progress report about his recent reconciliation with his alcoholic wife and how he was working the steps.

When the man sat down, Josh felt all the eyes in the room on him, closing him in. He studied his fingernails. He'd come to learn not to teach. Besides, what did he have to share that would help anyone else?

The chair scraped the floor as he pushed back from the table to give himself some breathing room. But it didn't help. The desire to get the meeting over and leave, as much as anything, propelled Josh to speak. "Hi, I'm Josh."

"Hi, Josh."

He crossed his arms. "I'm Connor's brother. My father is an alcoholic." He dropped his arms. "And I just found out two days ago that my girlfriend is a recovering alcoholic." Connor's side glance stopped him.

"Friend, girlfriend, close friend." Josh stumbled on. What did the name tag matter? He gave a factual recap of Thursday night, leaving out the emotion. Or, at least he thought he had.

"That's tough, man. Give the pain up to God," one of the group members said.

Some of Josh's darkness lifted. God knew his pain. These guys, especially Michael, did, too. "That's it. Thanks for listening," he said.

"Thank you, Josh. Anything more?" the leader asked. "No? Then let's close. We say the Serenity Prayer," he said for Josh's benefit.

"Courage to change the things that should be changed, and the Wisdom to distinguish the one from the other," Josh repeated with the others. "Living one day at a time, enjoying one moment at a time… Trusting that You will make all things right, if I surrender to Your will, so that I may be reasonably happy in this life, and supremely happy with You forever in the next. Amen."

He heard Connor stand beside him. "Coming?" his brother asked.

"In a minute." Josh leaned his elbows on the table, folding his hands, and rested his forehead against them. The surrendering he got. Rescuing, changing his relationship with Tessa, was going to take more courage than he had confidence he possessed, especially with his father in the picture. As for the wisdom, he couldn't think about that right now, not concerning Tessa. And taking things one day at a time. Him, the man who had his life all planned out for the next ten years, if not further? A life, he'd realized tonight, that he'd assumed Tessa would be in, wanted her to be in.

He felt a hand on his shoulder. "Powerful stuff," the group leader said.

"Yeah, and all I can do is pray for the ability to use it without messing up."

"One step at a time."

"Right." *But some of those steps were killers.*

"Tessa." Josh's voice in the hallway between the sanctuary and the church hall stopped her almost as short as it had Thursday night after the meeting. Only, it was anger, not heart-stopping terror today. *Make that anger and disappointment.* After not answering her calls and texts, he had the nerve—or lack of nerve—to face her in public? Ever since his father had come back, Josh wasn't the man she'd thought he was. Walking the short distance between them felt like slogging through cement. Maybe he never had been.

"Josh, I didn't see you in church. You must have come in after Grandma and I did." She parroted his words from the other night.

"I wasn't in church, or in the sanctuary, at least."

"Afraid?" she taunted.

"Scared straight." He attempted a grin.

Tessa took that as remorse for his behavior, but it wasn't enough to forgive his rude refusal to talk when she'd needed to talk with him.

"Are you free? We could catch some lunch before you have to be at the theater. Talk." His voice trailed off.

"No, I'm not." The bleak expression on his face washed away the brief self-satisfaction she'd gotten from her words. "I'm helping Grandma with coffee hour today and should get in there." She dragged herself away from Josh, pretending she hadn't been as harsh in not accepting his reach-out as he'd been in not even acknowledging hers.

Tessa nearly ran into Josh's stepgrandfather, Harry Stowe, in the doorway to the kitchen. "Cheer up," he said. "You look like you've lost your best friend. It's Sunday. The weather is beautiful." He waved a handful of paper towels. "And I'm about to rescue a table of lovely women from a vicious coffee spill."

She pasted a smile on her face and watched him weave around chairs to a table where his wife, Edna, Marie Delacroix and another of her grandmother's friends sat. She had lost her best friend and had no idea how to find him. One thing was sure. Hurting and avoiding him as he'd hurt and avoided her wasn't the way.

"There you are," her grandmother said.

"Sorry. I got sidelined."

"No problem. The food and drinks are out. All that's

left to be done right now is to take the bag of old trash out to the bin so we have room for the new trash."

She lifted the black garbage bag from the can, tied it up and put a new bag in. The warmth of the late-morning sun welcomed her when she stepped outside. She breathed in the fresh spring air hung with the scent of pine. Exactly what she needed to reset her mood, as she suspected her grandmother had known when she gave her the task. Tessa tossed the bag in the bin, closed the lid and started back across the parking lot, stopping halfway to retrieve her vibrating phone from her skirt pocket.

She didn't have to look at the ID to know it was Josh. Her finger hovered over the answer icon. He shouldn't be calling from the road. She lowered her finger. That was what she'd do. Answer and say she'd call him back later when he wasn't driving, put herself in control of the conversation when they had it. Or as much in control as she could.

"Hi, you shouldn't be calling when you're driving. I'll—"

"I'm not."

A horn honked behind her, making Tessa jump and her heart drop.

"Wait there. I'll drive over."

So much for taking control.

Josh rolled his truck over into the parking space next to her. "We need to talk," he said through the open window.

"Here?" She looked to either side and behind her.

"No, later. Come with me to Harry's birthday party this afternoon. We can walk up the mountain to Crystal Flow, where we had that picnic last summer with my brothers and Becca and Hope."

Tessa remembered. Lexi had been there, too. Josh had broken things off for good with her after the rest of them had left. "You know I have to work."

"Myles and Kaitlyn will cover for you. I already texted them."

Typical Josh. He had an answer for everything, too often an easy answer. But she couldn't see any easy answer to Thursday night.

"I'm not sure about Crystal Flow." A romantic setting wouldn't change the truth. She was an alcoholic, and he had no tolerance for alcoholics. She never should have let their friendship develop as far as it had. She kept others at a distance. Why hadn't she done that with Josh? They'd just clicked in a comfortable way, and he'd slipped into her life and her heart.

Josh leaned out the window, his confident expression bringing out the best in his already handsome features.

As if I had a choice in that matter.

"The party, then. Come to the party. I'll swing by and pick you up early. We can talk on the drive over to Gram and Harry's."

"I'll ride with my grandmother."

"Then you'll come." He slapped the top of the steering wheel. "I'll get back to Myles and Kaitlyn. And wear walking shoes in case you change your mind about the mountain."

"I'll talk to Myles and Kaitlyn," she said, ignoring his shoe advice. "The theater is my responsibility." And part of that responsibility was her and Josh finishing the renovations they'd started on it. She had to insist on a strictly business owner-contractor relationship between them. *Unless he can accept who I really am and not who he wants me to be.* And she had little hope of that.

* * *

Tessa stood on the Stowes' deck and smoothed the skirt of the very feminine retro sundress her grandmother had encouraged her to wear to the party. It was her mother's, from one of the boxes that had been in the garage apartment, and back in style. She looked over the backyard, where the guys had all congregated, leaving the women inside. Her original jeans and short-sleeved plaid shirt would have been a more comfortable choice. But the day had turned unusually warm and Grandma had looked so nice and spring-like in her green linen sheath.

She spotted Josh with Harry next to the brick grill at the far side of the yard and walked in that direction, the soft blades of spring grass brushing her toes. At least she'd stuck with her Tevas, so her feet would be comfortable, if not the rest of her.

Josh's voice drifted to her. "When Mrs. Hamilton and Tessa get here, do you mind if Tessa and I disappear for a while? I thought we'd hike up to Crystal Flow."

She pursed her lips. She'd told him that she didn't want to go to Crystal Flow. Tessa stopped. Well, more specifically, she'd said she wasn't sure about the hike.

"We'll be back in time for dinner," Josh said.

"It's fine with me, and I'll cover for you with your grandmother. She thinks it's time you fixed whatever is wrong between you two anyway." Harry winked at him.

How did the Stowes know? Tessa shook her head. Time to make her presence known. Tessa stepped past Josh and gave the retired high school principal a hug. "Happy Birthday, Mr. Stowe."

"Thank you. And you look exceptionally pretty today. Doesn't she, Josh?"

"Um, yeah. Nice dress." Josh scuffed his athletic shoe against the grass.

Tessa smiled at Mr. Stowe's compliment and Josh's discomfort.

"It's turned into such a nice day," the older man said. "Why don't you two take a walk and enjoy it? We won't be eating until an hour or so."

Tessa restrained her smile at Mr. Stowe's covering for Josh with her, too.

"How much of that did you hear?" Josh asked as he took her hand and tugged her to the empty middle of the yard.

"Of which part? Us hiking to Crystal Flow despite what I said or us fixing what's wrong between us?"

The bright sun highlighted the tint of pink on Josh's tanned cheeks. "Let's go with would you like to take a walk and talk? I can't stand the wall between us."

"I can't, either, but taking it down won't be easy."

Josh repositioned their hands and laced his fingers through hers. They walked in silence across the grass to the break in the woods behind the yard where the trail started. While a part of her welcomed his touch, it didn't help her jumbled nerves. The undeniable physical attraction was new to her. But she could handle it and was onto Josh's usual kiss-it-and-make-it-better approach with women. It wouldn't work with her. Attraction wasn't enough to dismantle the wall and repair their friendship. And she'd learned from her mistakes. Friendship— like Josh's brothers and their wives had, Grandma and Grandpa had, even her parents, despite their other faults, had—was what she wanted in a relationship. Friendship, trust and love.

From Josh. The thought whispered on the breeze rustling the budding tree branches overhead. *Don't even go there; you know where loving someone who can't love the real you leads.* The face of her former fiancé breaking their engagement flashed in front of her.

"You're awfully quiet for someone who agreed to talk."

"Collecting my words, thoughts." *And storing the personal ones away.* "We have to maintain at least a business owner-contractor relationship until the theater renovation is done. I can do that."

"What if I want more?"

Her pulse quickened. *Lord, please help me not give in.* They reached the flow and the bench Harry had built on the edge of his property overlooking the water.

Josh dropped her hand and motioned her to sit, giving her some time to pull herself together. He sat beside her, not touching.

"Is the answer that hard? I thought we were friends." He ran his hand over his hair. "Sure, Thursday threw me for a loop, and I acted like an idiot ignoring you. I'm sorry."

She lifted her hand from her lap to brush back the lock of hair that had fallen on his brow, stopped herself and placed her arm on the bench's armrest.

"I'm ready to move on," he said.

"Are you?"

His eyes darkened at her challenge.

She cleared her throat and stared unblinking at the rushing waters until her eyes watered. "If you knew all about me when we met, would we still have become friends?" Tessa held her breath as the seconds ticked by.

"No," he said in a low voice.

Her breath whooshed out, along with the glimmer of hope she'd held inside. "Thanks for being honest."

Josh placed a finger on her cheek and turned her face

toward him. "But I'm working on that. I went to another meeting with Connor. I listened. I shared." His voice hitched. "About you. I'm learning. One day at a time."

She gripped the armrest. More than anything, Tessa wanted to lean into Josh, feel his strong arm around her shoulder. "So you're working on accepting that I'm a recovering alcoholic and you can't change that. What about your father?"

Josh tensed. "This is about you and me. He's different."

"No, he's not. I'm an alcoholic. Your father is an alcoholic. Yes, we're different people. But we're both alcoholics going it one day at a time. I've gone two thousand and two days. When I spoke with him at church, he'd gone three hundred and ninety-seven days."

"That was this morning." Josh smirked, adding cement to the wall. "On my way over here, I saw his truck parked in his old drinking buddy Ray Sinclair's driveway."

Ray was in the program, too. She'd met him at both of the meetings she attended regularly. But that wasn't for her to share.

Tessa pinned Josh's gaze with hers. "Either of us, *either* could have a relapse today, tomorrow, next week. Until you accept that, work on healing things with your father as well as me, I can't let us be more than business partners." Her voice caught despite her best efforts to keep it strong and unemotional.

Josh's pupils dilated until they were almost black, and a muscle worked in his jaw. He leaned closer, drawing her to him like a magnet and setting off an almost nauseating flutter of anticipation and fear. Their lips touched, his questioning, hers answering with what she felt rather than what she'd reasoned. He rested his hands on her waist and she automatically raised her arms and placed them around his shoulders before she caught herself. She pushed him away gently, the effort nearly draining her already depleted resolve.

"That doesn't change things," she said.

"I know, as much as I wish it did. But it can't be undone, and you can't say our kiss didn't affect you."

"No, I can't say it didn't affect me." *More like rocked me to my core.* "But we can't repeat it."

"Is that what you want?"

She dropped her hands from his shoulders. "Being this close to you, I don't know what I want." Her heart tripped when she saw no triumph on his face.

"Tessa, I'll try with Dad if it will help you and me."

She held firm. "It has to help you."

"I'll try. It's all I can say."

"And pray, pray hard and listen to Him. That's what's gotten me to where I am." Although she hadn't heard many clear answers lately.

Josh nodded. "I hear you." He stood. "We'd better head back before Gram sends my brothers looking for us."

He offered her a hand up and she took it. As much as she thought she should avoid his touch again, she knew they were both too fragile right now to brush away his offer. She let him pull her to her feet and squeezed his hand before she dropped it.

Josh gave her a wobbly smile that opened a crack in her armor just wide enough to let the glimmer of hope for them she'd lost earlier slip back into her heart.

Chapter Ten

Josh was barely in the front door of Jack and Suzi Hill's house the next evening when Owen had him by the hand and was dragging him through the front hall. "Coach Josh, I have everything all set up for us in the workshop in the basement."

"Slow down. Let me check in with Mr. or Mrs. Hill. And were you supposed to open the door without one of them in the room?" That was one kid rule they hadn't had at his house, but he'd picked up on it from Jared and Becca.

Suzi appeared in the doorway of the living room. "No, although he did shout that you were pulling in."

"I recognized his truck." Owen faced Suzi. "I knew it was him."

"House rules," Suzi said.

"I know." Owen dropped his chin to his chest. "I'll remember next time."

"Okay. I told Owen earlier that the brownies I'm baking should be done and cool enough to sample when you guys are finished. They'll be in the kitchen." Suzi went back into the other room.

"Brownies are one of my favorites," Josh said.

"Me, too." Owen glanced back at the window. "Is Coach Tessa coming to help us?"

"No, it's just us guys."

"Oh, okay. The workshop's this way," Owen said.

He followed Owen through the kitchen and down the basement stairs, his curiosity getting the best of him. "Why did you ask about Tessa?"

The boy jumped off the last step and shrugged. "You always come to soccer together, and sometimes you sit with her at church. And the last time Mom took Dylan and me out for pizza, you and Coach Tessa were there getting pizza."

Owen made them sound like a couple. Was that how everyone saw them? Everyone but Tessa. His heart dropped. He'd be fortunate to work his way back to friend status. "Ah, I'm helping her do some work on the theater. When we get hungry, we go over and get pizza."

"Do you do the hard stuff for her, at the theater?" Owen walked to Jack's workbench and scrambled up the stool beside it. "My mom says she misses having a guy around to do the hard stuff. So I try to help her. But I think she just misses Daddy like I do. Hope said your daddy went away, too. Did you miss him?"

What was it with Owen and questions? Or, he thought about Hope, was it all kids and questions? He scratched the back of his neck. "I was a lot older than you when my father went away," he said, as if that was an answer. "How about you show me the car kit so we can get started?"

"I've already got all the pieces out here." Owen swept his arm down the workbench.

"Got any ideas what you want it to look like?" Josh asked.

Owen's eyes sparkled. "A cool, fast race car."

"I thought you might say that." Josh whipped a folded paper out of the back pocket of his jeans and spread it in front of Owen. The little boy looked at Josh's drawing and gave him a wide smile.

"Did you make this with the computer program you showed us at school?"

"I sure did."

"Cool! Mr. Hill said the saw we need is hanging up there." Owen pointed at a coping saw on the wall behind the bench.

Josh lifted the saw from the hooks and breathed a silent sigh of relief that he'd diverted the conversation from Tessa and fathers. Josh understood that the little guy might need to talk, but he wasn't the person to talk to. Not about fathers. That was way out of his element.

"Hand me the pencil and the straight edge," he said.

"You mean this ruler?" Owen asked.

"Yep. I'm going to make two lines to show us where to cut the wood, here and here." Josh ran his finger across and down the wood block that would be the body of the car. He looked at his diagram and drew the lines. "Ready to make the first cut?"

"You're going to let me, by myself?"

"It's your car. You have to do the work." Josh stepped behind Owen. "Put your hand on the front of the block." He placed his hand over the boy's. "Here's the saw. Stop here." Josh pointed to the intersection of the two lines he'd drawn.

"I pull it back and forth like this, on the line, right?"

"You've got it."

During the minutes it took for Owen's short back-and-forth motion to cut through the block, Josh went back in time to another project, a birdhouse for a fourth grade science project. Dad had stood behind him, just as he stood behind Owen, guiding him in cutting and nailing together the pieces. After they painted it and hung it in the tree next to the garage, Dad had taken him—only him—to get a kid's meal at a fast food restaurant in Ticonderoga. Then, one night the next week, after a pair of robins had laid eggs in the birdhouse, Dad had drunkenly stumbled into the birdhouse, knocked it down and kicked it across the yard, putting an end to the robins and the project and the memory of the fun they'd had.

"Done," Owen said, stopping his sawing where Josh had shown him to.

The boy's smile shot through Josh, warming and saddening him. He'd have to be happy with this and being a big brother and uncle. There was no way he'd ever be a real dad. Not with the fear he held inside that he might parent as his father had.

Josh helped Owen slide the saw out of the cut.

"What I sawed is going to be the spoiler, right?"

"Right." *The spoiler.* That's why he couldn't accept Dad, as he was trying to accept Tessa. Dad always ended up spoiling everything good, and Josh couldn't let him spoil him and Tessa.

Owen flexed his fingers. "My hand's tired. Can you do the other cutting?"

"Sure." He figured other fathers—and mothers— must help their kids. Besides attacking the wood block would work off some of the resentment his memory had kindled. In no time, the triangular woodcut curving up to Owen's spoiler fell to the bench top.

"That was fast," Owen said.

"Hey, you want to get to the fun part, painting and detailing, don't you?"

Owen bobbed his head up and down in agreement.

"I want to paint it red. My daddy had a red Charger. It was fast. He had to sell it to pay Dylan's doctor's bills."

Owen's father might be a felon, but it sounded like he'd taken more responsibility for his family than his old man had. Dad had let everything fall on Mom. Josh squeezed the bridge of his nose. *Unbelievable.* He was jealous of a little boy whose father was in prison and mother was in a coma in the hospital's intensive care unit.

"Red's good. What do you say to black details?"

"Yeah! Will we get to paint it tonight?"

Josh studied the rough-cut block. "Not tonight. All the edges need to be sanded smooth like in my drawing. I'll show you how, and then I think it's time to go test Suzi's brownies. We can paint next weekend, Saturday after the soccer game."

"All right."

A few minutes later they were upstairs at the kitchen table with two brownies each in front of them and big glasses of milk Owen had poured.

"Can I ask you a question?" Owen said between bites.

"Shoot," Josh said, expecting something about the car.

"Hope says you don't like your father since he came back. Do you think when I'm bigger and Daddy comes back I won't like him anymore?"

Josh choked on his mouthful of milk. Shouldn't Owen be talking about stuff like this with the Hills? They had foster parent training. He couldn't tell the kid he'd never liked his father. *No, that wasn't true.* But he hadn't in a long time.

"Your situation's different."

Owen eyed him with a solemn expression.

"My father just left us. We didn't see him for years and years."

"Yeah, Hope told me she never saw him before he moved here."

"You see your dad. You told me you and your mom moved here so it would be easier to go see him."

Owen nodded. "And I write him letters about school and soccer, and I'm going to send him a picture of my race car when it's done. Mom and Dylan and I pray for him, too. She said she thinks it's working. The last letter we got, Dad said he'd gotten a Bible and was looking up all the verses Dylan and I told him we're learning in Sunday school."

"That's good." The brownie Josh had eaten sat in his stomach like a lead bullet.

"Mom says we'll be okay when Dad gets out. We just have to be *positive* and *encouraging* until then."

"Your mom's a smart lady."

Owen smiled. "You could try being positive and encouraging to your father."

Like Tessa keeps telling me. Josh stared at Owen for a moment, feeling as if the boy was the adult and he was the child.

Suzi poked her head in the kitchen. "Time to get ready for bed, Owen."

Josh rose, glad he'd dodged having to respond to Owen. "Work on that sanding so it's finished by next Saturday afternoon."

"I'll have it done."

"Good man."

Positive and encouraging. Owen's words stuck with Josh as he let himself out. If only he could hold on to the good memories like Owen and not let the bad ones crush them. If Al-Anon and God could show him how to do that, maybe he could support his father and bury his fear that Tessa might become one more of Jerry Donnelly's casualties.

Tessa's heart bled for the two little boys who stood by the graveside at the Hazardtown cemetery behind the church, clutching the hands of a tall, dark-haired man in leg irons. Two New York State Correctional Officers flanked him, overseen by the county sheriff and a deputy for good measure. A tear ran down her face and Josh squeezed her hand he held in her lap. Letting him take her hand had seemed so natural, even though she was trying to discourage anything personal between them unless he could come to terms with his father.

Pastor Connor finished the service with the twenty-third Psalm. "Surely goodness and love will follow me all the days of my life and I will dwell in the house of the Lord forever."

The man and the boys stepped forward, and Connor handed Owen and his brother each a white rose. They let go of their father's hands, took the roses and placed them on their mother's grave. Their father dropped to his knees. The correctional officers lurched toward him, and the sheriff and his deputy rose from their folding chairs. Connor waved them back as the man rested his hands and forehead on his wife's casket.

"He's not going anywhere," Connor said.

The officers allowed him his grief. Rhys Maddox straightened and hugged his boys to him before standing and allowing the officers to lead him away.

"Those poor babies," a woman behind Tessa and Josh said.

"That poor man," Josh said for Tessa's ears only.

"I'm glad Connor was able to help Jack and Suzi get permission for him to come."

"Me, too." Tessa unwrapped her hand from Josh's and wiped another tear from her cheek. "Are you coming back to the church? The ladies' group is having a light lunch, as they usually do for the families. Or do you have to go in to work?" She reached for her purse on the ground beside her seat.

"I took the whole day off. I need to be there for Owen. He's my little buddy. I hope they put the guy who did this to him behind bars for a good long time."

The intensity of Josh's words chilled her.

"What?" he asked.

"Let's leave the judgment to God."

"You're right." He stood and looked into the distance. "I thought I'd stain the new floor at the Majestic this afternoon, since I have the time. It'll make up for tomorrow afternoon, when I told Owen I'd help him finish his race car. Want to help me?" he asked, focusing back on her.

The uncertainty in his eyes undid her. "Sure." *It was business*. "I didn't know you and Myles finished the new floor."

"Yeah, we worked late last night. It looks great, if I do say so myself."

"I wouldn't expect any less." She and Josh followed the other mourners to the church.

"What do you think will happen to Owen and his brother?" Josh asked.

"Suzi says for now, they'll stay with her and Jack. Their father has an appeal coming up. Evidently, there's some new evidence about the robbery."

"So that's what he's serving time for. I didn't know." She touched his arm. "But don't say anything to

Owen. The counselor the boys are seeing thinks it's best not to get their hopes up about the possibility of their father being released early."

"You know me better than that."

She did. Despite Josh's protests that he didn't know anything about kids, she knew he wouldn't do something he thought might hurt Owen.

"I have enough experience having fatherly expectations dashed. I certainly wouldn't get Owen's hopes up about his father unless it was a done deal."

"Sit," she said, pointing at the block and stone wall around the Memory Garden on the church side of the cemetery. The funeral had catapulted her seesawing emotions about Josh and her and his father into a tailspin. "I've had all the 'poor little Josh' I can take."

He had the grace to look chagrined. They sat on the wall and waited for the people who'd been walking the path behind them to pass.

"I meant it when I said I'd try with Dad, try to forgive him. Maybe I should have gone to the meeting last night." His gaze searched hers. "But I like the Saturday night one better."

"I'm not counting your meetings or approving your choices. That's your journey," she said.

"You're not going to give me any slack, are you?"

"How much slack have you given your father?" Tessa bit her tongue, expecting him to get up and leave. No, go inside. Josh wouldn't leave without seeing Owen.

Josh rubbed his face with his palms and released a harsh laugh. "Monday night Owen shared some advice from his mother. He told me I should try being positive and encouraging to my father." The vulnerability in his expression when he raised his head stopped her questions before she could ask them.

"He got to talking about his father being gone and my father being gone." Josh rambled on as if he had to get the words out or explode. "I remembered a good time I'd had with Dad working on a birdhouse, like Owen and I were working on his derby car. I was feeling good until I remembered the ugly corollary to the good time." He told her about his father destroying the birdhouse.

"That's harsh. But you aren't the only one who's had disappointments."

"I know that."

Tessa took another plunge. She had to if she and Josh were ever going to have the future she was beginning to think they could have. "You know that rationally. But emotionally, you've collected all those disappointments into a big pile that you hide behind. In front is the 'show' Josh you let people see and in back is the real Josh. Know which one I like?"

"The one in the back."

"Both, if you'd clear out the garbage in between."

"Then you'd like me twice as much?" He grinned.

She slugged his shoulder. "I'm serious. Read your Al-Anon literature. Pray. Start clearing out the garbage."

"You're a good friend and I don't want to lose you," Josh said. "But I don't know if I can throw off the compulsion to protect what's good in my life…" He shook his head and dropped his chin to his chest. "To protect you from my father. I couldn't live with him ruining you, like he's ruined so many other things I've wanted."

Josh's words warmed her with the hope he wanted their friendship enough to forgive his father and allow himself some faith in Jerry's recovery—and not just hers. Because he'd never seen her drink, drunk, didn't mean she was any better than his father was. She cleared her throat. "We're the only ones who can ruin our friendship. And I have no plans to."

"So you wouldn't be averse to my sticking around Paradox Lake?" he asked.

Her pulse ticked up. "What do you mean?"

"There may be an opening for a project manager at the Ticonderoga office. No details yet." He pushed off the wall. "All this talking has me hungry. We'd better get inside before all the food is gone."

She slid to her feet. No, despite her remaining uncertainties about Josh being willing to accept his father and fully accept who she really was, she didn't mind him sticking around for a while. She gazed through her lashes at him standing straight and tall like the soldier, protector, he'd been and still was, waiting for her. She touched her finger to her lips. The truth be known, she wouldn't mind another one of his kisses, either.

"No meeting tonight?" her grandmother asked when Tessa entered the living room and sat to watch the news with her.

Tessa bristled. First, Josh's concern about his father hurting her, endangering her sobriety. Now her grandmother was counting how many times Tessa went to meetings? Since Tessa had come out of rehab more than five years ago, her grandmother had taken Tessa's direction and been hands-off about her recovery. Why the concern now? She'd thought she'd been keeping things together pretty well, considering the turmoil of the past week, especially when it came to Josh.

"I didn't mean to pry," her grandmother said. "I'm set in my routines and not used to you being here Thursday nights. You're usually either at the singles group or AA."

Tessa's shoulders sagged. Grandma wasn't prying.

She was making conversation. "It's Josh," she blurted. What was she thinking? This was her grandmother. Who talked about their love life with their grandmother? How sad was she that she didn't have a girlfriend she felt close enough to confide in? But she did. Her sponsor, Maura. But Maura couldn't answer the questions that had taken Tessa's thoughts hostage. Only someone who'd been in Josh's situation could, someone with an alcoholic family member.

Her grandmother patted her knee. "You two seemed to be getting along at Harry's birthday party."

Tessa straightened and scraped one thumbnail against the edge of the other. "I think I may want more than getting along."

"About time."

"What do you mean?"

"You've been friends for how long, five years?"

"About that."

"And when was the last time either of you went out with anyone else?"

Tessa tilted her head and thought. Josh hadn't really seen anyone since he broke up with Lexi last summer. And, not counting her no-show blind date for the Resurrection Light concert, she didn't know when she'd last gone on a date. "A while."

"Why would I be surprised that you two have feelings for each other?"

"I don't know that Josh does beyond friendship." She remembered the sweet kiss they'd shared. But that might have been Josh being Josh.

"I've seen the way he looks at you when you're not watching."

Her heart skittered and slammed into her internal wall. "Before we can move beyond being friends, we have to get back to being friends." She hesitated. "I told him I'm an alcoholic." Tessa replayed that night for her grandmother, Josh seeing her leaving the AA meeting with Maura and Josh's father when he walked out of the Al-Anon meeting and what happened when they'd talked afterward.

Her grandmother bit her lip, as if stopping herself from speaking. A couple of years ago she'd told Tessa that she should be straight with Josh. But only that once.

"When we talked again at Harry's birthday party, Josh didn't really believe what I'd said, that I was like his father. He'd never seen me drink, let alone drunk. Josh has to accept that I *am* like his father and his father is like me. We both want to stay sober. But no one but us can guarantee we will. I can't let Josh into my heart any more than I already have until I'm sure he accepts me for who I am and his father for who he is now."

Her grandmother opened her arms and Tessa sank into her hug. "Josh isn't your former fiancé," her grandmother said. "I watched him grow up. He's a much bigger man."

"I know." Tessa drew back. What she couldn't trust was that he was big enough to fully accept everything and commit himself to their relationship. "How did you accept me when I was such a broken mess? You and Grandpa must have been disappointed in me. I know Mom and Dad were. I just couldn't pull myself together."

Her grandmother's lips thinned. "But you did pull yourself together, even if it wasn't the way your parents expected you to, and you've moved forward."

"With a lot of help from Maura and the others and the former Hazardtown Community pastor. But you didn't answer my question about how." Knowing that might help her open Josh's eyes to remembering the father of his early years, the father he'd once loved, and she was certain still did.

"We prayed and did our best to love you unconditionally as our Lord does and put you in His hands. It wasn't easy. It was heartbreaking at times to watch you fall. But each time, we prayed ourselves out of stepping in and enabling you or losing faith that He'd guide you."

Tessa wiped the moisture from her eyes. "I think Josh can do that for me as a friend. But Gram." Her voice caught. "I don't know if that's enough to build anything more than friendship." *At least not until he sees and accepts his father, too.*

"Honey, you won't know until you try."

"And if I fail?"

"You'll go on and find your happiness elsewhere. You're one of the strongest people I know."

Tessa stared at the TV, not hearing a word the newscaster was saying. But was she strong enough to risk their friendship to bare her growing feelings to Josh and reconcile him with his father?

Chapter Eleven

Josh put the finishing touches on his design and hit Save and Close. He'd have just enough time to grab something to eat and get to Owen's Pinewood Derby at the church. Owen had asked him and Tessa to come cheer him on. She was planning to meet him there after she got Myles and Kaitlyn set up for the Friday movie showing.

His phone dinged a text message at the same time Anne Hazard poked her head in his cubicle.

"Go ahead," she said, motioning to his phone.

You're still going to Owen's race, right? Jack texted.

Our evening driver's out sick, and I got a call to help clear a fender bender up near Ticonderoga. Dropping Owen off at the parsonage. Not sure when I'll get back. Suzi and Dylan are down with something, probably what my driver has.

On it, Josh texted back.

"What's up?" he asked Anne.

"Do you have a minute? I wasn't sure I'd catch you since it's Friday, and you've been coming in early."

He gave the computer clock a sidewise glance, thinking about Owen. *About a minute.* But Anne was the owner of GreenSpaces. If she wanted to talk, he was talking.

"I stayed to finish the design for the addition to the Ticonderoga Birthing Center."

Anne pulled the side chair over to his desk and sat. "I was going to tell you Monday morning, but this way you'll have the weekend to celebrate—I hope."

Josh's pulse raced with anticipation.

"I approved the new project manager position here, and we'd like you to take it."

He bit back the Yes! shout that sprang to his tongue. "Thank you."

"I don't need your answer now. I know you'd expressed an interest in transferring out of the Ticonderoga office. Think about it. Talk it over with Tessa and your family."

He started at Anne's mention of Tessa. Everyone thought of them as a couple, except them. But she would be the first person he talked with. He'd already mentioned the possibility to her.

"Yes, I'll do that. When do you need my answer?"

"The end of next week would be good. If you don't take it, HR will have to start a search for someone. I want to have the position staffed as soon as possible to cover the additional late spring and summer work we always have."

"Sure, no problem." Project manager was the next step in his planned career path. He was almost ready to take the job right now—if only he had his head as straight about Tessa as his heart, had a better feel of where he and Tessa were headed. Of course, he could take the job and put in for a lateral transfer when a project manager position opened up somewhere else in the company. *Yeah*. Get the experience and the higher pay scale.

"Good," Anne said. "I'd like to see you in the position here." She stood. "Now, I've got to get going. Alex has his Pinewood Derby tonight."

"Me, too. I helped Owen Maddox build his. He's a friend of Hope's."

"And Alex's, too. See you later, then."

When Anne was out of earshot, Josh slapped his desk. "All right!" He shut down his laptop and almost collided with his father as he exited the cubicle.

"Congratulations," his father said. "I couldn't help overhearing." He gestured to the wall facing the cubicle. "I was setting up to paint."

"Thanks." Josh's excitement closed the distance his bitterness usually put between him and his dad.

His father nudged the paint can on the floor with his toe. "I'm proud of you. Your military service. Finishing your college degree while working full-time. I'm proud of all three of you. Your mother did a good job."

"She did." For once, Josh didn't feel a need to color his father's acknowledgment with a dig about Mom having to do it all because Dad wasn't there. *One day at a time*.

"I'd better get back to work," his father said.

"And I've got to get the Cub Scouts' Pinewood Derby. I helped Owen, Hope's friend, with his racer."

"He's sure latched on to you. I've seen him and you at coffee hour at church. You're good with him and with Hope. You'll make a good father someday, like your brother Jared has."

Josh ignored the bubble of longing expanding inside him and let his father's remark hang. He had to get to the derby. "See you, Dad."

"Yeah, and unless I have my guess wrong, your job news is going to make someone else happy, too."

Tessa. The bubble burst, and bile rose in his throat. He didn't like his father assuming he was familiar enough with Tessa to know what would or wouldn't make her happy. He thought about his father and Tessa attending the same meetings and forging the bonds he was with the members of the Saturday Al-Anon meeting. Josh liked the idea that his father might be that familiar with her even less.

His stomach grumbled as he strode across the GreenSpaces parking lot to his truck. Inside he grabbed the two protein bars he kept stashed there for when he was working in the field and couldn't stop for lunch at the usual time. They weren't his idea of dinner but would hold him until after the race. The church hall was teeming with noise and prerace activity when he entered. He spotted Tessa with Owen right off, and Owen sped over.

"Coach Josh, I was afraid you weren't coming. Mr. Hill said he texted you. I had Coach Tessa text you again and you didn't answer."

Josh blinked in amazement at how the kid got all of that out in one breath.

"My boss stopped by my workstation and wanted to talk with me before I left."

Tessa joined them, raising an eyebrow before breaking into a broad smile. Maybe his father was right. Tessa's kiss at the funeral did mean she wanted him to stay here.

"I'll tell you later," Josh said.

"When I'm grown-up, I'm going to be my own boss like Mr. Hill is, except for his father. So I can do what I want. Maybe I'll be a race car driver or ride motocross like your brother."

"You've got time to decide," Josh said with a chuckle. He glanced at Tessa. If Owen only knew how much bosses, even self-employed ones, had to answer to others. "Have you looked over our competition?"

"We did." Owen nodded solemnly. "Ours looks the best."

"You did a good job with it. We'd better get a seat before they're all taken."

The corners of Owen's mouth drooped. "We had ones by the finish line. I hope no one took them."

"I've got that covered. Neal Hazard said he'd save them for us," Tessa said.

"Good work," Josh said. "Lead the way."

Owen darted ahead to his seat in the front row with Alex Hazard. Anne greeted him with a smile he couldn't read but that made Tessa blush. Had they been talking about him before he'd arrived? *Nah.* Not with Neal sitting right there. Or would they? He shifted to get comfortable in the metal folding chair.

"You raised the bar on this competition," Neal said.

"How's that?"

"Alex came home from school talking all about how you and Owen designed his car on the computer. We had to do the same."

"Gotta play your strengths."

"Sanding and painting weren't Alex's. He lost interest. Owen's car looks a lot sharper. He said he did all the sanding and painting himself."

"That he did."

"My hat's off to you for getting him to."

Josh sat back in his seat and crossed his arms with self-satisfaction.

"What are you grinning at?" Tessa asked.

He stretched his legs out as far in front of him as he could. Neal and Anne had three kids, and from all appearances, Neal was the kind of father any child would want. Yet, he'd been able to "out-father" Neal and keep Owen's interest in the project, thanks to his big brother and uncle experience. But he wasn't going to tell Tessa that, not here, probably not at all.

A call for the first heat to line up saved him from Tessa pursuing her question. Owen's and Alex's cars both made it into the semifinals, competing in different heats, which kept everyone on the edge of the seats and cheering for both cars. They groaned in unison when Alex's car lost his semifinal heat.

"Did you see that?" Owen turned around and shouted at Josh and Tessa when his car slid ahead and won his heat.

"I saw," Josh said, nearly as excited as Owen.

Owen's and the other two cars in the final heat were lined up. "On your mark, get set, go," the race announcer said, sending the cars into action.

"Mine's ahead," Owen said, jumping up and down. "Go!"

Josh joined him. "Go, go!"

At the last second, one of the other cars inched ahead and crossed the finish line first.

"So close, buddy." Josh patted Owen on the back.

"It's okay," Owen said with a wan smile.

"And now for the awards," the announcer said.

Owen beamed when the announcer called him to receive his second place trophy and even more when his car won ribbons for both best craftsmanship and paint job. "Look at that." He waved the ribbons. "I think when I'm done being a race car driver, I'm going to design cars. What do you think, Coach?"

"It's a plan," Josh said.

"I wish my mom…"

Josh's heart ached when Owen stopped and looked at Josh and Tessa and Jack, who'd made it for the semi-final heat.

"It's okay to wish she were here," Tessa said, leaning across the back of his chair to hug the little boy.

"And you can write your dad, like you were telling me about," Josh said.

"You and me?" Owen asked.

Josh shoved his hands in the front pockets of his Dockers. "I think that's something for Mr. or Mrs. Hill to help you with."

"Right," Jack said. "We have the address."

"I'm going to tell him all about the race, and soccer and you, Coach Josh."

Josh pushed his hands in farther. He didn't want the man to think he was trying to take his place. Nor for Owen to depend on him as a father-substitute. Parenting Owen was Jack's place.

"Don't forget Coach Tessa," Josh said.

"Right." Owen grinned at Tessa.

"Time to get going," Jack said.

"Okay," Owen said. "See you guys at soccer tomorrow. I'll be there early to help set up the cones, Coach Tessa."

Tessa's mouth twitched as she tried to keep a straight face while she checked out Owen's enthusiastic offer with Jack. He nodded.

"Fifteen minutes early is good," she said.

Josh's gaze remained on Tessa while she watched Jack herd Owen ahead of him to leave. She was good with kids, would make some kids a good mother. His father's words—that he'd make a good father someday—echoed in his head. Him, Tessa, kids. What was he thinking? He was the good-time guy, the fun uncle, the guy who worked the fast track to have the dollars to impress the ladies and buy his niece and nephew and Hope the stuff Jared and Becca wouldn't. He wasn't father material and, sadly, his head told him, not what Tessa wanted and needed, what she deserved.

"So, what were you going to tell me?" Tessa asked as they walked out to their vehicles.

"Anne stopped by on her way out of work to tell me she'd approved the addition of the new project manager position I told you about."

"And you're still under consideration for it?"

"Yes."

"Here's hoping." Tessa raised a fist to him as she climbed into her car.

Coward, the wind shouted at him.

"Hey, bro, you here to lend a hand?" Connor shouted from the parsonage front lawn before he shut off the mower and met Josh in the driveway. "I've got the church yard to do after the house. The church's volunteer groundskeeper is away for the weekend."

"You're busy." Josh reached for his truck door handle to hop back in.

"Not that busy. What brings you here so early on a Saturday morning?"

Josh flicked the door handle up and down. "I wondered if we could talk."

"Sure." Connor motioned to two Adirondack chairs on the front porch. "As your brother or as your pastor?"

Josh released the handle and looked at the house. "A little of both."

"Dad's not here," Connor said, following Josh's gaze.

"I know. He's at GreenSpaces, painting."

"Go ahead." Connor settled in the farther chair.

"Anne offered me a promotion to a new project manager at the Ticonderoga office."

"That's good or not?"

"You know I want the job. I don't know about sticking around here."

"Does Tessa know?"

Josh slapped the arm of the chair. "What is with everyone and Tessa and me?"

Connor shrugged. "She's usually the person you talk to."

Josh relaxed. "I told her there's going to be an opening, not that Anne offered me the job."

Connor didn't say anything, which set Josh to tapping the armrest with his fingers. "When I told Tessa, she said she wouldn't mind me sticking around. But there are things. Tessa's past."

"And present."

"And present and future. I'm working on that part." Josh deflected Connor's barb.

"And Dad." Connor poked him.

"And Dad." Josh acknowledged the five-hundred-pound gorilla in the room. "He overheard Anne offering me the job yesterday and congratulated me. He said he was proud of me, of all of us."

"I think he always has been."

Josh couldn't agree. He remembered too many times when their father hadn't been aware enough of them to be proud or anything else. His conscience pricked him.

"We talked a little. It was okay." Okay, as long as he didn't think of Dad and Tessa together.

"That's progress," Connor said. "One day at a time. The same for you and Tessa." Connor's gaze darted to the door. "Natalie had some things in her past that were an obstacle to our getting back together when she returned to Paradox Lake."

"You never said anything to me." Josh stopped. "But you did to Jared." His words sounded like an accusation. Josh fought the long-standing sibling rivalry between him and Jared and the hurt that after how hard he'd tried to be there for Connor after Jared left, Connor had turned to their older brother instead of him.

"Jared and Becca…"

"Were happily married," Josh finished, "and I was drifting, playing the field."

"I'm sorry."

"It's fine. What I need to know is how you got by those obstacles."

"After a sufficient number of stupid blunders, mostly on my part, and some serious prayer, we both put them behind us and left them there in the past."

"I want to do that for Tessa. With Dad, too, for her." Josh ignored the frown Connor gave him when he said *for her*. Connor's expecting him to forgive their father, as if half their childhoods hadn't existed, was asking too much.

"All right. Big questions. Do you love her?"

"We're best friends."

"Not what I asked. Do you love her?"

"Seriously. How would I know? I've never loved anyone but you and Jared and Mom and Gram. I have feelings for Tessa."

"Friendship and feelings are a start."

"Are they enough? Tessa, all women, have expectations I don't think I can fulfill."

"Don't sell yourself short, big bro. Test the waters. Tell Tessa about the promotion. See what she thinks."

Josh checked the time on his cell phone and pushed up from the chair. "I've got to get over to the school. Our game is at eleven today."

"Okay. Think about what I said."

Josh nodded. "You… Natalie had problems. Almost didn't get together?"

"You've got it. Talk to Tessa. And pray for guidance."

"This." Josh pointed his finger back and forth between himself and Connor. "Between us only. I can still take you down one hand tied behind my back if I want to."

"So you think."

"So I know."

Josh got to the soccer field as the earlier game was finishing. He climbed to the top row of the bleachers away from everyone else and watched the clouds overhead break away into blue sky. Josh took Connor's advice and bowed his head. Connor was the man, even if he was his little brother.

Lord, please help me see things clearly and give me a direction, along with the strength to follow that direction. The thought that his path might be a life without Tessa shot through him like a careening bomb set on annihilation. *Even if I don't like where Your direction is taking me.*

When he raised his head, Josh spotted Tessa crossing the grass to the field, the equipment duffel flung over her shoulder. He took a moment to admire her athletic grace before bounding down the bleachers.

"Hey," he called. "I thought you'd see my truck in

the lot and text me to come help with the equipment." He reached for the duffel.

"Think I can't handle it?" She feigned a duck away from his hand.

He caught hold of the cord and she released her grip. "Not for a moment," he said.

When they reached the field, he dropped the equipment bag on the ground next to the bleachers and flexed his fingers.

"Is something wrong?" Tessa asked.

He waited until the last person from the earlier game passed them. "No, something's right. Anne didn't just tell me about approving the project manager position yesterday. She offered it to me."

"But last night—"

"I wasn't ready to tell you. I needed to process things."

"Your father being here?"

"And a lot more." He studied her face. Did she realize he meant her, them?

"Is it what you want?"

"I think so." Both the job and Tessa. "It's a good opportunity for advancement, and I like the people I work with."

"But you're not sure. You've been talking about leaving the area for a position with GreenSpaces elsewhere since the day we met, more so lately."

Josh heard Tessa's comment as unspoken concern about his relationship with his father. That, or he was too fixated on it himself. Why was he waffling? He could handle his father. The move to project manager was what he'd been working toward the past three years with his Utica PolyTech distance learning courses. "No,

I *am* sure. On Monday, I'm going to tell Anne I accept the job."

Tessa clapped and threw her arms around his shoulders in a quick hug. "I'm glad. Congratulations," she said, releasing him.

His gaze dropped to her lips. *So close.*

She stepped back at the sound of children's voices in the background. Hope and Owen were racing across the grass, arguing, his father following behind.

Josh shook his hands to unfreeze the tension that immediately infused his every muscle. He could only hope the congratulations on his decision weren't premature.

A burnt smell drifted from the kitchen, bringing Tessa at a full run from the dining room where she'd been arranging daffodils, tulips and violets from her grandmother's flower gardens. What was she thinking, inviting Josh to a home-cooked celebration dinner when he'd texted her this morning that he'd accepted the promotion? She didn't cook.

Her spaghetti sauce—made from jar sauce with a few extra ingredients her grandmother had suggested—bubbled over the side of the pot to join the puddle on the stovetop that was running onto the burner. She grabbed a pot holder and the big metal spoon from the utensil holder above the stove and sighed with relief when a few deep stirs to the bottom of the pan assured her the only burnt sauce was the stuff on the stovetop. After wiping up the spill and turning on the exhaust fan above the stove, she put water on to boil for the pasta, the last thing she needed to do. Tessa checked the clock and admired her masterpiece cooling on the counter—a strawberry-rhubarb pie, Josh's favorite, made from his grandmother's recipe. She'd called Mrs. Stowe, who'd graciously shared it. The salad was in the refrigerator. Everything was set.

"Mmmm. It smells good in here." Tessa's grandmother sniffed the air as she entered the kitchen. "When is Josh coming?"

"I told him six."

"Marie will be by about quarter of to pick me up."

Knowing her grandmother had plans for the evening had seemed perfect this morning when Tessa had asked Josh over. Now, thinking back over the week and the awkwardness of her growing attraction to Josh, she wondered if there wouldn't be more safety in numbers.

"No rush. I've made plenty if you and Mrs. Delacroix want to eat with us before you go to your meeting."

"I wouldn't think of it," her grandmother said. "If you want, I'll put the pasta in so you can change."

Tessa looked at her sauce-spattered T-shirt and jeans. Everything was set, except her. She hadn't even thought about what to wear. Preparing the food had taken all her concentration, and it wasn't as if she usually gave any thought what to wear to hang with Josh. But tonight didn't feel like just hanging out.

"That would be great," Tessa said.

Her grandmother lifted the pan lid to see if the pasta water was boiling. "I washed and dried that heather top that looks so nice on you, along with the skirt you often wear with it. They're up on your bed."

"Okay. Thanks." She'd gotten several compliments on the crocheted-lace-trimmed T-shirt and flowing calf-length skirt when she'd worn the outfit to church. But it was kind of dressy for her everyday wear. She expected Josh would go home and change into jeans before coming over.

"Scoot," Grandma said. "Or he'll be here before you're back down."

Then she wouldn't have to decide what to wear. Of course, Grandma had already done that for her anyway. She walked upstairs. Her usual jeans and a blouse would be fine. Why was she obsessing about what to wear anyway? Josh probably wouldn't notice what she had on. She opened her bedroom door and saw the clothes her grandmother had laid out on the bed, along with Tessa's amethyst pendant and matching teardrop earrings. But she wanted Josh to notice. She wanted to feel pretty for him, make him see her as more than a buddy.

Tessa quickly showered, put on the softly feminine outfit and jewelry and ran a hairbrush through her chestnut waves. She pulled her hair back to pin it up in a knot as she usually wore and stopped, releasing the strands to cascade over her shoulders. *No.* Tonight was a celebration. She'd wear it down. Josh had told her she looked nice when she wore her hair down for Connor's wedding. She added some mascara and lipstick and twirled around in front of the mirror, sending the gauzy fabric of the multicolored skirt swirling out around her knees. Now she was set, too. As set as she was going to be.

On the way downstairs, her heart thumped with anticipation, tempered by a longing to cross back over into just-friends territory. She moistened her lips and swallowed the phantom taste of Chianti in her mouth, a reminder of the Tessa Josh had to recognize and accept if they were going to move forward to test the relationship she wanted.

"Hey," Josh said when Tessa reached the doorway from the stairs to the living room.

His gaze rested on her until she wondered if she'd put her top on inside out or something.

"Your grandmother let me in on her way out and said you'd be right down."

Tessa waltzed off the last step. "Well, here I am."

"So you are. You look pretty. I like your hair like that."

"Thank you. You look nice, too." Josh had dressed up, too, or not changed from his work clothes. *No, no way his Dockers would have held a sharp crease like that all day long.*

Tessa smoothed her skirt and lowered her gaze to her bare feet and Barney-the-Dinosaur-purple toenails.

His gaze followed. "Nice touch." His mouth curved in a warm smile that stopped short of being his typical grin.

She felt her cheeks pink. What was wrong with her? He'd certainly seen her feet before. "I'll just go slip on my shoes. They're in the kitchen." She'd left her wedge pumps by the door after church yesterday. "And check on dinner."

Josh rose. Shoeless, she felt diminutive beside him. "I'll come give you a hand."

"Of course. You didn't think I was going to wait on you, did you?"

"Never." Josh followed her into the kitchen.

"The plates and cups are in the upper cupboard and the flatware is in the drawer next to the sink." In companionable silence, Tessa put the pasta and sauce in serving bowls and placed them on the table while Josh put out the place settings. She grabbed the salad from the refrigerator.

Josh surveyed the table when he'd finished. "I'm starving. Is that everything? It all looks and smells delicious."

"Because you're starving?"

"No, because it does. And is that a strawberry-rhubarb pie there on the counter by any chance?"

"It is. I got the recipe from your grandmother." Which she hoped assured her success, since it was the first pie she'd ever baked.

"Home-cooked food. Pie. You've gone all out," he said.

"It's not every day we have something this big to celebrate."

Josh's eyes flickered before brightening, interrupting the reassuring camaraderie that had been guiding Tessa into a familiar comfortable rhythm with him.

"Yep. College done. Check. Project manager job. Check. I aced it again, right on schedule."

Tessa laughed. "With that, I think it's time to get your mouth doing something other than talking." She reached for the back of her chair, but Josh got there first and pulled it out for her with a flourish. "Thanks," she said. "Now sit."

Once Josh was in the chair across from her, Tessa bowed her head. "Dear Lord, thank You for this food and the opportunities You have given both of us." She paused for a nanosecond. "Right here. Use us to Your service. Amen."

"Amen," Josh said, picking up his fork and taking his time swirling the spaghetti around it.

"It's safe," she said. Josh was fully aware of her cooking abilities and lack thereof.

He completed the spin. "It's not that." As if to prove his point, Josh shoveled in the forkful of spaghetti.

Tessa fingered her pendant. Was he having second thoughts? As long as she'd known Josh, he'd been talking about leaving the Paradox Lake area.

"I have to go to the Boston office for a couple of

weeks to shadow one of the project managers there as training. Even though I won't be starting the new manager position here until they hire a new drafter to replace me, Anne wants me to leave first thing tomorrow morning. The manager I'm going to shadow will be on vacation for a couple of weeks beginning week after next."

"You don't sound very enthused."

"I am. It'll be great to get some hands-on direction and see how a larger office operates." He placed his fork on his plate. "It's the Majestic."

Tessa waved him off with relief. "Not to worry. You've got the new wiring done, except for the kitchen area you partitioned off and the stage lights. We can all pitch in on getting the new wallboard up in there once you get back and wire the kitchen. Myles and I can handle the taping and painting. After you get back, we'll still have a couple of weeks until the opening."

Josh released his breath in a puff. "It's not the wiring or the walls. It's the stage floor. I was looking at it yesterday, to get Myles going refinishing it to match the new dining floor. I found what looks like old carpenter ant damage to some of the under flooring and support beams."

"Oh. Did you go ahead and call an exterminator? You didn't have to wait and clear it with me."

Josh nodded. "They're coming Wednesday. But that's not the real problem. The stage isn't safe. It has to be rebuilt."

"Can Myles and I work on it while you're gone?"

"You can tear down the old stage, but I need to be here for the construction."

Tessa bit back an argument. Josh wouldn't have said that if he thought she and Myles could handle the work without him. He wouldn't put his ego ahead of getting the work done.

"I'll get revised plans to the town zoning board before I leave for Boston tomorrow."

"Josh, it's okay," she said with more bravado than she felt. "Put it away for now. We're celebrating. To your new job." She lifted a meatball in toast.

"To my new job." He did the same.

"We'll just have to work double-time on the theater when you get back."

Josh gulped down some water. "About that. With the new job, I'm not going to be able to take as much vacation time as I'd planned to work on the theater."

She cleaved the meatball in half with her fork. He wasn't going to bail on her now that he got his promotion, was he?

"But don't worry. I'll blank out all my evenings and Saturdays for you and ask Myles if any of his friends want to pick up some work. We'll make your planned Memorial Day weekend opening." He reached across the table and squeezed her hand. "You and I have too much going between us for me to let you down. Not after the way you've put up with me all these years and been there whenever I've needed you."

Tessa let his words flow over her and squeezed his hand back, caressing the callused palm. "You do know I'm not infallible?" she asked, not quite achieving the lightness she wanted.

Silence hung for a moment.

"Yes, I understand what you mean and accept it."

"Do you?" She might as well lay her heart open. "Because I think we're on the edge of something special."

His face lit as if her words had lifted a burden from him. "So do I. No one is perfect. You have your inner demons. I have mine. With God's help, we can overcome them together. I think it's a battle worth fighting."

Josh's admission was more powerful than even her grandparents' unconditional support. "With troops like that," she said, "how can we lose?"

Chapter Twelve

The manager job was everything Josh had expected and wanted. The people he was training with in the Boston office were great, almost as great as his co-workers in Ticonderoga. Not seeing Tessa for eleven days was another story. They'd talked on the phone almost daily, but late at night after Tessa had finished working with Myles at the Majestic. And it wasn't the same as talking in person and seeing her expressions. He'd admit, to himself at least, that he had it bad. But not bad enough to suggest Skypeing, not enough to let her know how much he yearned to see her smile. This new road they were taking was still under construction. He hadn't identified all of the possible land mines yet.

Josh's cell phone *choo-chooed* an alert to a text message from Hope, pulling him from his thoughts and bed.

Where are you? We're done setting up the field.

Josh blinked and refocused on the phone screen. *Eight-forty. The match was at nine.* When he'd glanced at the alarm clock a few minutes ago, he'd thought it said seven-thirty. He stretched. After going out to dinner with the guys from the Boston office, he hadn't even started his four-hour drive home until after nine last night.

Better get a move on it. He started grabbing clothes. This was the championship game he'd boasted that the team would make at the beginning of the season. What kind of coach would be late for the championship game? Not the kind he wanted to be, nor the kind he realized he'd been all season.

"About time," Hope shouted before he'd even reached the field, drawing the attention of the people on the bleachers.

He strode to her and Tessa and ruffled his sister's hair. "The game doesn't start for another five, and I'm sure you and Coach Tessa have everything in hand."

"Late night with the drive home?" Tessa asked.

"More like early morning." He stopped himself from rubbing his eyes. "The guys wanted to take me to dinner before I left."

Josh scanned the front bleachers for the usual Donnelly contingent and didn't see them. "Where are Jared and Becca and Connor and Natalie?"

"Don't you remember?" Hope asked. "Brendon has his big motocross race today at Jared's track. He gets Jared, Becca and Natalie. I get you, Connor and Daddy, except Connor got a phone call and is going to be late."

"I did forget." Josh laughed at the way Hope and Brendon had divvied up the family and rechecked the bleachers. "How did you get here?"

"Daddy."

"Where is he?" *If he'd just dropped Hope here and left...*

"Way up there." She pointed to the top corner of the bleachers. "He didn't know he was supposed to sit in front, and I had to help Tessa, so I didn't tell him yet. Mr. and Mrs. Hill are saving seats for him and Connor."

Josh shielded his eyes from the bright morning sun and found his father sitting alone in the top left-hand corner. "I'll tell him."

The smile Tessa flashed him confirmed that he'd actually spoken the words. He raced up the stands in double-time before he thought of a reason not to.

"Hey, Dad."

"Josh. Isn't the game about to start?"

He glanced at the field below. "Yeah, but didn't Hope and Connor tell you that the Donnellys all sit front and center?" He could set aside his ill feelings about his dad for the morning—for Hope, for Tessa.

"I…"

Josh waved off any argument his father might have. "Come on. I've got to get back down." His father matched him almost bound for bound down the stands. *Not bad for an old guy.*

Tessa gave Josh a hidden thumbs-up as the Hills welcomed his father, and he took the seat they'd saved for him. Josh scuffed the toe of his athletic shoe in the shorn grass between the bleachers and the field, glad that the referee's shrill whistle signaling the teams to take the field prevented Tessa from saying anything.

The kids played fierce and fast, ending the first half with the score tied zero to zero. Josh and Tessa fielded dirty looks from some of the kids and spectators, along with a few jeers from the stands, when they rotated in the less-skilled team members after the half. They'd agreed ahead of the game that everyone on the team deserved to play in the championship.

With minutes left and the score still tied zip-zip, the opposing team got in a bullet shot that looked to be a sure goal. Owen raced from the left of the goal where he'd fielded the last attempt and propelled his compact little body like a rocket to the right side of the goal, knocking the kick out and landing facedown on the field. Before the referee could whistle a stop to the game, Owen leaped to his feet and waved that he was okay, a move that gave Hope time to get the ball and dribble it down the field into scoring range.

Josh grabbed Tessa's hand without a thought of all the people watching and sucked in a breath as Hope eyed the goal and held the attention of the other team's goalkeeper. Then Hope gave the ball a sharp kick to the right, passing off to her friend Sophia, one of the substitute players. Sophia slammed it into the right corner of the net. Half the bleachers went wild, and Tessa hugged him and jumped up and down. Anyone who didn't already see them as a couple before would now, and that didn't bother him a bit—at least not at the moment.

The ref waited until the crowd quieted and restarted the clock at forty-five seconds. The opposing team kicked off. With the ball halfway down the field, the timer went off.

"We won!" The Hazardtown Hornets raced off the field and circled Tessa and Josh, Hope, Owen and a few others hugging their legs.

"What did I tell you before the season started?" Josh shouted to the mini melee surrounding him.

"That we're champions!" the kids shouted back.

"And you are, each and every one of you," Tessa said, surveying the circle.

Josh's heart nearly burst when he noticed that she spent an extra moment on the second-string players. Tessa was so beautiful inside and out.

"Line up, guys," Josh said. "Let's show the Tops Tigers they were worthy opponents."

The team walked out, formed a line adjacent to the Tigers' line and started walking down shaking their opponents' hands.

"Good game." The opposing coach—someone neither Josh nor Tessa had met before soccer season—walked over and shook their hands. "The dark-haired girl. She your daughter?" he asked Josh. "She looks like a pip."

Josh felt a tug to claim Hope as his. "No, my little sister, and she is a pip."

"Get you next year," the other coach said.

"We'll take that as a challenge."

"Congratulations." Connor and his father slapped Josh on the back, distracting him from the direction his thoughts were straying, to next year and Tessa.

"You and Tessa make a great coaching team," his father added.

Josh flung his arm over Tessa's shoulders. "Did you expect any less?"

His father's quiet "No," sent Josh's thoughts back to Tessa, the future and the kids. Maybe, like his brothers, he did have the whole marriage, kids and happily-ever-after somewhere deep inside him.

"Hey, team, everyone." Josh caught the kids before they started leaving. "What do you say you check with your parents and see if you can meet Coach Tessa and me at the soft serve stand on Paradox Lake for an ice cream cone? My treat."

"Yay!" they shouted as they took off to ask their parents.

Josh glanced at Tessa talking with his father. The absence of the knee-jerk protectiveness he usually felt anytime his father got near her startled him. He took off his ball cap, ran his hand over his hair and replaced the cap. He'd mull over the meaning of that and his earlier thoughts later when he'd come down from the rush of the past couple of weeks and his head was clear. For today, he'd assume his usual carefree MO and just enjoy himself.

"Tessa, you want to go for coffee?" Jerry Donnelly caught up with her as she left the Elizabethtown meeting Thursday night.

Her gaze darted to the open door of the empty Al-Anon meeting room, searching for Josh. Tessa wasn't looking for any surprises like the last time she'd been to the meeting here, not when things between her and Josh were going so well. They'd worked on the stage construction every evening this week. Today he'd texted that he had to work late. She'd told him that was fine. She'd work on the wall taping with Myles and they could catch up on Saturday when all three of them were there. Then, this afternoon, she'd been overwhelmed by an ominous feeling that everything was going too well and had called Maura, who'd suggested a meeting.

"Coffee—well, tea for me—would be good," she said. "Anyone else coming?"

"No. I have something I wanted to talk over with you. I'll meet you there."

Over the short driving distance to the diner, Tessa's mind wouldn't stop trying to second-guess why Jerry wanted to talk with her. It kept circling around to Josh. He hadn't said anything to her, but last Saturday at the game, he and his father had seemed to have come to some kind of truce. Tessa wasn't sure she could talk with Jerry about Josh, not without violating Josh's trust, and she wouldn't do that. Her loyalty was with Josh.

Jerry met her at the door and, when they were inside, asked for seating in a booth in the back. She slowly followed him to the booth, stopping to acknowledge some of the other people from the meeting along the way. She slid in across from him.

"What's up?"

He unwrapped flatware and arranged it on the table in front of him. "We live nearby, attend the same meetings…"

Tessa relaxed. This wasn't about Josh at all. Jerry probably wanted to share rides to meetings, or it could be something about the garage painting. But the painting was done, and her grandmother had been the one who'd hired him, not her.

"What can I get you tonight?" the waitress asked.

"I'll have tea," Tessa said.

"Coffee for me, and was that strawberry-rhubarb pie I saw on the way in?"

"Yes, it was."

"I'll take a slice."

The waitress added the pie to their order. "I'll be right back."

"Josh is a fan of strawberry-rhubarb pie, too," Tessa said.

"So is Jared," Jerry said. "Edna makes the best."

"Yeah, she gave me her recipe to make one for Josh. But you didn't ask me here to talk about pie."

"No." Jerry leaned back in the booth so the waitress could place his coffee and pie on the table. "You know my sponsor lives in Saranac Lake."

She didn't, but nodded anyway to see where he was going.

"He thinks it would be a good move for me to have a sober support buddy closer."

"You're looking for suggestions?" Tessa's mind inventoried the guys she knew who attended the meetings she and Jerry did. "I know you and Ray are old friends, but he's probably too recently sober."

Jerry sliced the tip off his pie and moved it around the plate. "I have someone in mind."

"And you want my input," Tessa said, as if she could reroute where she thought he was going.

"Tessa, I don't want input. My sponsor suggested you. I'm asking you if you'd consider being my sober support." He raised his hand to stop her from saying anything yet. "I admire you and your sobriety. We live minutes away from each other. Hey, we're almost family," he joked.

That was a big almost. And with Josh seeming to think he needed to protect her from his father, spending time with Jerry wasn't the way to draw her and Josh closer.

"I meant you and Josh coaching Hope's team...and everything."

Her face must have given away her uncertainty about being his sober support and about her and Josh.

"Think about it," he said. "I don't need to know right away."

"I will." *And pray hard.* She finished her tea in silence. "I'd better get going. I've got to be over to the Majestic bright and early so Myles and I can get in some work on the renovations before showtime."

"How are they coming?"

"Pretty good, except Josh found carpenter ant damage, and that means we need to replace the stage. Myles and I tore out the old one while Josh was in Boston, and Josh and Myles and I have been building the new one this week."

"That's tough. Your grandmother said you wanted to be set to open the dinner theater Memorial Day weekend."

"Barring any more unforeseen delays, we should be able to."

"Before you go," Jerry said, "let me give you my phone number, so you can get back to me when you decide about the sober support."

Tessa pulled out her phone. "Ready." He rattled off the number and she punched it in her contacts. "I'll be talking to you."

"Maybe I'll swing by tomorrow and take a look at the work you've done at the theater when I pick up the paint your grandmother let me store in her garage."

"Sure." Not that it should matter, although somehow it did, Josh had a rush project he had to finish at Green-Spaces so only she and Myles would be there.

When Tessa got home, her first thought was to call Josh. He was her usual go-to person for decisions. But he wasn't exactly a bipartisan sounding board for his father's sober support request.

"Is that you, Tessa?" her grandmother called from upstairs.

A nervous giggle bubbled up inside her. What would her grandmother say if she replied, *No, it's a burglar who jimmied the lock and let myself in.* She took a calming breath. "Yeah, it's me."

"Okay, see you in the morning." Tessa checked the back door, shut off the lights and went up to bed.

After a restless night that three cups of coffee with her breakfast didn't wipe out, Tessa dragged herself to the Majestic at eight o'clock. From the sidewalk, she spotted Myles and Kaitlyn ready and waiting by the back door. She frowned. Not to throw cold water on young love or turn down free labor, but she hoped Kaitlyn wasn't staying. Wednesday when she'd come by after classes ostensibly to help Tessa and Myles, the girl had spent most of the time acting helpless and asking Myles to "show me how."

"Hi, guys," Tessa said.

Myles turned and she saw his right arm in a cast held by a sling.

"What happened to you?"

"After last night's movie, Kaitlyn and I went over to the school field where some of the guys were playing midnight football." Myles spoke to his feet. "I kind of tripped and fell and broke my arm."

"Trespassing. Playing ball in the dark. What were you thinking?"

He shrugged. "It sounded like fun when the guys texted me."

"You're okay?"

"Well, it's broken and will be in a cast for at least four weeks. Kaitlyn drove me over to see what we can do together to help. I know you're on a tight time frame for the opening and all."

Tight was right—only sixteen days until the scheduled opening on Memorial Day. Tessa thought about the advertising she'd already started and paid for and the reservations she'd taken for opening night, not to mention the food arrangements and local players she'd hired. They wanted to do at least the dress rehearsal at the theater.

"No, that's okay," she said. She could probably get more done on her own. "I'll talk with Josh, and we'll come up with something"

"I'm really sorry," Myles said.

"I know. Take care." Tessa let herself in, walked over

to one of the theater seats and dropped into it. What was she going to do? Myles had come up short on any friends looking for work, except Kaitlyn.

"Tessa?" The morning sun lit a male silhouette in the doorway. She jerked to her feet. She hadn't even heard the door open.

"The door was ajar. I thought I'd better check it," Jerry said, as her eyes focused him in. "What are you doing sitting in the dark?"

"Getting my work crew—me—ready to start." She walked back to the door and reached past Jerry to flick the light switches on.

"I thought Myles was helping you."

"He managed to break his arm last night, horsing around with his friends."

"Oops. I don't have anything lined up for today if you want me to stick around and help you."

"I can't pay you."

"I didn't ask you to. Think of it as my giving back to the community."

She considered the progress she and Josh had been able to make on the stage Tuesday, Wednesday and Thursday evenings and how much was left to do. Josh might not like it, but it wasn't Josh's theater. "When you put it that way, how can I refuse?"

"I don't have any work lined up during the day next week, either, just a painting gig Friday evening."

Tessa weighed whether to see Jerry's work today first against the way that might sound to Jerry and the need to get the job done. "You've got work now," she said.

His return grin, so much like Josh's, hit her with a double shot of relief and apprehension.

Working with Jerry was a lot like working with Josh. It made her wonder if some of the friction between them was because they were too much alike. She gazed at Jerry measuring and remeasuring the lumber for the stair risers before making a cut. Except for alcohol, and maybe there, too. As far as she knew, Josh never drank, hadn't even experimented with it as a teen. Could it be he subconsciously sensed it was a weakness in him, or did she want that to be the case so he could understand her and his father?

"Want a drink?" she asked near quitting time when the buzz of the circular saw Jerry was using stopped.

Jerry looked up and blinked.

"A soft drink. I can go out to the lobby and get us each a cup. Then why don't we call it a day?"

"Sounds good." He pulled the saw plug from the wall. "Make mine a large cola."

"Got it."

A couple of minutes later, Tessa pushed the inside theater door in with her hip and turned to see Jerry and Josh facing off on the dining floor.

"What are you doing here?" Josh demanded.

"Helping me," Tessa said.

Josh looked toward the back of the theater to see her tearing down the center aisle juggling two large cups. "Where's Myles?"

Tessa brushed by him and handed his father one of the cups. His father nodded thanks.

"I'd guess Myles is home nursing his broken arm," she said.

"Myles broke his arm? How?" Concern drained some of the protective outrage he'd felt at expecting to surprise Tessa with an offer to pick up burgers before showtime tonight, and seeing his father instead.

"Tessa, I'm going," his father said.

"I'll see you Monday at eight," Tessa said.

His father tapped the brim of his cap.

"What's that about?" Josh asked. "A meeting?" He hated the way the last two words came out as almost a snarl. If only it wasn't his father who'd stepped in to help Tessa today. So much for the absence of malice he experienced at the game last week.

"Your father's free during the day next week and volunteered to help me here. He told me to think of it as giving back to the community."

"Do you think that's wise?" Josh asked. *More amends. The old man was grasping that with two hands, not that he didn't owe a lot of people around here.*

"What do you mean? You can see how much we got done today."

Josh looked at the completed work. *Yes, that was the problem.* All he could think of was that his father could give Tessa a full day's work every day and he could only give her a couple hours an evening and Saturdays. And, with today as an example, he couldn't guarantee Saturdays. Josh tried, but couldn't crush the feeling that the theater was his and Tessa's project. The feeling that his father was taking it from him as he'd taken much of his childhood by abdicating his family responsibilities, leaving Josh and Jared to shoulder them.

"It'll take some of the pressure off you," she said. "You know with the new job in the wings and getting all your drafting projects completed."

He could live with the pressure to get more time with Tessa. "I still have those vacation days scheduled. I can run them by Anne again."

Tessa's face lit with surprise, as if she knew what he was offering. But then she said, "Thanks, but your new job comes first. Jerry and I can handle things."

His job had always come first, until now, and she was brushing that off with a *thanks, but your father is just as good*. Maybe he—or anyone—was in this case. Josh had always focused on his job, his career and making money flipping houses. He was on solid ground there, knew he was good at what he did. As for relationships, he'd never gotten past mastering the superficial. Tessa knew that as well as he did. His logic told him it was time to step back into the friend zone and do some reconnaissance, while the rest of him wanted to be the white knight swooping in to rescue Tessa and her theater project.

"Okay." Josh gestured with one hand. "Here it is. I don't want you to depend on my father and be disappointed when he doesn't show and the work falls behind."

"I don't think I will be." Tessa touched his arm. "Your picture of him is too colored by the past. I know him as he is now."

She thought she knew his father better than he did? He wanted to laugh and shake off her hand, but pathetically he couldn't give up the reassuring warmth. Nor could he bear to hurt her with the truth she wouldn't accept. "I have a bad feeling about you spending so much time with him."

She drew back her hand, leaving a cold spot beneath his flannel shirtsleeve where she'd touched him. "Sit with me." She led him to one of the tables. "I like your father. He reminds me of you in some ways."

Josh bit his tongue to not interrupt. He was nothing like his father. He'd built his life on not being like his father.

"We work together well, like you and I do. He understands my past in a way that I'm not sure you do." She stopped and looked at him, her dark eyelashes framing her warm gaze. "I know you're trying to."

He thought he did understand.

"He respects me and what I've accomplished."

"You don't think I respect you?" Josh didn't care that he let the hurt show in his voice. "You're the most beautiful, talented, compassionate woman I've ever known."

Tessa blushed. "I meant about my addiction. He asked me to be his sober support buddy."

Josh had read about sober support in his Al-Anon literature and the slogan, "I can't stay sober, but we can." Although he hadn't seen anything to the contrary yet, Josh didn't think his father could stay sober for good, singular or with a whole regiment of others behind him.

"You told him no."

"No, I'm considering it."

Josh gripped the edge of the table. "You can't. You don't really know him. I told you, he ruins everything he gets close to. And I can think of only one way he can ruin you."

"You mean ruin your vision of me."

"No." He lifted the table a half inch and dropped it. "Dad will start drinking and drag you down with him, like he did to us, only worse. He'll steal your sobriety."

"You don't trust me." Tessa's voice was barely above a whisper.

"No, don't you see? I don't trust him, and neither can you."

"I have to until he proves otherwise."

"And he will. Tell me you won't be his sober support."

"I can't. I'm praying on it and have to go with His answer."

Josh turned to leave.

"Will you be here to work Monday evening?" Tessa asked. "I'll be viewing the new movie trailers."

He spun back around and surveyed the work Tessa and his father had accomplished today. "I don't know that you and Dad need me to be."

"Come on, Josh, grow up."

He knew he was being childish and petty. But it tore him apart that Tessa couldn't see the truth, his truth. His father and his father's *problem* were overshadowing his life again, soiling the good he'd worked for and found once he'd finally gotten free of him.

"I'll let you know about Monday," he said.

Once outside, he leaned his forehead against his forearm on the top of the driver's-side door of his truck. Maybe Tessa had hit the nail on the head. As much as he wanted to, he didn't trust either one of them—or himself and his feelings, either.

Chapter Thirteen

Tessa wrestled with Jerry's request to be his sober support and Josh's urging against it most of Saturday night and all day Sunday until she finally fell asleep Sunday night praying. She woke Monday morning no closer to an answer than when she'd gone to sleep, and headed over to the Majestic to meet Jerry. The minutes ticked by, eight-ten, eight-twenty, no Jerry. She started the wall spackling she could do herself, not wanting Josh to be right about depending on his father.

Her cell phone rang, and she dropped the spackling knife. "Hello," she said.

"Tessa. It's Jerry. I need your help."

Her heart leaped to her throat. Did his words sound slurred?

"I'm at Ray's. I called my sponsor and didn't get through."

She swallowed.

"Ray's in bad shape. The emergency squad just took him to the medical center. He called me before he passed out and hit his head on the corner of the kitchen table. He didn't want his daughter to find him like this. I called her, and she's meeting the ambulance at the hospital." Jerry stopped. "There's an open bottle of vodka on the table."

"Hang on. I'll be right there." She sprinted out of the theater without stopping to lock up. Ray lived on the side street behind the Majestic. She'd get there faster on foot. Her phone chimed Josh's ringtone. She answered automatically without breaking her stride. "Hi."

"Hey, I'm not going to be able to make it tonight," he said.

Her urgency to get to Jerry diluted her disappointment. "I can't talk. Your dad. He's at Ray's. I have to get over there. I'll call you back."

"I'll be on my way to Boston. Tessa, don't let him suck you in. Please. I care… I la…just don't. Okay?"

Tessa's heart tore in half. "I'm there. You have to understand. I'll talk to you later." She hung up and flung open the side door, the door she guessed opened into the kitchen.

Jerry sat at the table, staring at the bottle, his hands gripping the table edge so like Josh had Saturday at the theater, except Jerry's knuckles were white and his breathing harsh. She stood for a moment and felt his longing. No, her own longing, although wine had always been her poison of choice.

"Jerry. Pick it up and dump it down the sink."

"Tessa." He looked over his shoulder. "You came."

"I said I would. Pick it up and dump it."

Jerry stood, turning his attention back to the bottle. He picked it up and held it in front of him.

Tessa sucked in a breath. She'd come. It was his choice.

Jerry closed the distance between the table and the sink with one long stride and, hand shaking, tipped the bottle upside down. Tessa released her breath in a whoosh. He rinsed it out.

Tessa steadied her own hand before reaching toward him. "I'll put it in the recycle bin by the door."

"Thanks," he said. "You don't know how much I appreciate you coming."

"Of course I do." She sloughed off his words.

"Yeah, you do." He dropped back into the chair by the table.

"What's this?" She gestured toward him, palm up. "We've got work to do."

"Right." He pushed himself to his feet and followed her out, turning the lock on the inside door handle before he closed it.

"We've got a long day ahead of us," she said as they rounded the house to Jerry's truck in the driveway.

"I'm okay," he said.

"Not that. I talked to Josh on my way over."

Jerry frowned.

"I didn't call him. He called me. He's on his way to Boston and won't be able to work on the theater tonight. I don't know how long he'll be gone. I didn't get the details, said I'd call him back."

"I don't want to come between you two," Jerry said as he backed the truck onto the street.

"You aren't." She slumped in the passenger seat. "But if he can't reconcile with you, he can't truly accept me, and I can't be with him."

Jerry's arms tensed. A minute later he parked the truck behind the theater. "I'll get started on the work. You go ahead and call Josh. See if you can drill some sense into him. He's kind of hardheaded. Something like his old man in that."

"Kind of? I've frequently wondered if his skull is made of titanium."

Jerry laughed. "Don't give up on him. Even titanium isn't impenetrable."

Tessa left him and went to the lobby to call Josh. She sat on the chair behind the snack counter and listened to his phone ring.

"Hey," Josh finally answered. "I had to pull over to talk. I don't have my Bluetooth."

"Hi, your dad's okay. He went to help Ray and called me for backup." She gave Josh a brief recap and the line went quiet for so long she thought one of them had lost reception.

"I see," he said.

From Josh's tone, Tessa knew he didn't see at all. But now, on the phone, wasn't the time to rehash that. "What's up in Boston? More training?"

"No, the project manager I shadowed for training who was supposed to be on vacation came down with spinal meningitis. He's going to be out for weeks, so I volunteered to fill in for him. I can finish off my CAD projects there as well as in Ticonderoga or have the drafters at the Boston office finish them."

"So you'll be there awhile."

"Yes, but you're good for the theater opening, what with Dad there finishing up everything. I wouldn't have volunteered if I thought it would put you in a bind."

She heard the silent "you don't need me," behind his words, and it stung like a wasp bite. "This isn't some choice I'm making between you and your father."

"Feels that way to me. You've decided to be his support, haven't you?"

A weight lifted off Tessa as she realized she had. "I haven't told him yet, but I am."

"I'm not going to watch you destroy your life saving him like Mom did all those years. There's a permanent project manager position for me in Boston if I want it. You know that was my long-time goal before my father showed up or Anne created the new position here. Maybe I should stick with that plan."

Tessa shook her head in disbelief. "Is that some kind of threat? You'll run away to Boston if I associate with your father?"

"No." Josh's voice sounded old and weary. "You could come to Boston. GreenSpaces is going to have an opening for a civil engineer soon, or you could get involved with a theater here. We could make a fresh start. I know that I'm asking a lot. But I think I'm falling in love with you. Could you consider coming with me?"

Tessa's heart choked her. She *knew* she was in love with Josh, which made answering him all the harder.

"Never mind. If it takes you this long to respond, I know your answer. I've got to get back on the road."

"Wait," she said, but he'd already hung up.

Could she give up the theater for him? For all she loved the theater, she could for Josh's true acceptance and love. But unless he could give up protecting her from his alcoholic father, protecting her from herself, she'd never have that. And if she couldn't have Josh, she needed the Majestic.

The tracking page of the trucking service supposedly delivering the new stage lights read *Departed Syracuse. In transit*, the same as it had last night, first thing this morning and an hour ago when Tessa had called the destination office in Ticonderoga. She'd arranged for her and Jerry to pick them up there so they'd have them a day earlier than waiting for delivery to the theater. The truck from Syracuse had arrived in Ticonderoga, but not the lights. The Syracuse warehouse was checking to see if the lights were on another truck, although the woman Tessa had talked with had said no other trucks were scheduled for Ticonderoga today.

Tessa cradled her head in her hands. She should have gone with the in-stock lights instead of back-ordering the ones Josh had recommended. It was Wednesday. The lights had to be in tomorrow. The building inspector was coming by Friday morning to sign off on the last of the work. She couldn't cut it any closer for the Memorial Day opening.

Her cell phone rang and she jerked, almost knocking her iPad off the theater café table. *Josh.* "Hello."

"Hey, how's it going?"

How's it going? Just like that, just like he hadn't taken off for Boston a week and a half ago and called her only once, the next day, to say he'd contacted the attorney who'd drawn up their contract to use the termination clause to dissolve it. Josh had assured her she wouldn't owe him any royalties on the Majestic's future profits, and the attorney would have a check for her for the back rent on the apartment, as they'd agreed to in the contract if he couldn't complete the work for any reason. His assurances did nothing to alleviate her feeling that he was dissolving much more.

"Good," she said, putting up her guard. In contrast to today, he'd been cool and businesslike on his earlier call. She'd accepted that as of a week ago, they'd ceased to be partners in any way. Still, she'd had to stop herself more than once from calling him over the days following— about the work, something she'd seen that she knew he'd be interested in…just to hear his voice.

"Anne said Neal did the kitchen wiring for you."

The wiring you didn't do. "Yeah, last Friday for a summer subscription to the theater for him and Anne, and your brothers and father put up the wall board Monday. I finished the painting this morning.

"Everything's done?"

She was probably imagining it, but his voice sounded wistful. Or was he skeptical that she and his father had completed the work without him? "Except the stage lights. They go in tomorrow. Remember, I had to back-order them?"

"Once you have them installed, you're going to see they were worth the wait."

If they ever arrived.

Josh launched into all the reasons he'd recommended the missing lights. "I'll be there this weekend to see it all finished. I wouldn't miss your opening."

Before Tessa could process his excitement, her phone signaled another call, from the trucking company. "I've got to take this," she said. "I'll see you this weekend."

She took the other call. "Tessa Hamilton."

"Ms. Hamilton, we've located your shipment. It went to our Saratoga facility."

"Thank you. We'll be down in an hour or so to pick them up."

She phoned Jerry and, while she waited for him and his truck, she replayed her conversation with Josh and what bothered her so much about it. Josh had been his usual jovial self. *That was it.* Josh had talked to her in the verging-on-superficial flirty way he talked to everyone else. She slumped in the chair. They really were finished.

Josh thought he'd pulled off his conversation with Tessa the other day. He'd been upbeat, friendly, kept it light—all while he was dying inside, thinking about his dad helping Tessa with the work he should have been doing. From what Connor had told him, his dad had been there for Tessa when he wasn't. The two weeks he'd spent in Boston earlier in the month training had been fun. He'd known he was going back to Tessa. The past week and a half had been torture, thinking he wouldn't be. Was he ever glad he'd cooled down and not put in for the project manager position in Boston.

If he could only figure out what he needed to do to prove to Tessa he did love her. He could take the bad with the good. His evenings alone in his hotel room had given him lots of time to think about him and Tessa and about the rest of his family. They'd had good times with their father when they were young and older, too, Josh had to admit. And Mom's choices had been hers. She'd never asked him and Jared to run interference for her. That had been their own doing. She'd accepted her husband, failings and all, and her choices. Mom was happy. Josh rubbed his chin. He didn't need to protect Mom now, hadn't for years, maybe never. It had been his need, not hers, and he'd transferred it to Tessa as soon as his father had returned. He'd held on to his anger at his father. He loved Mom so he'd tried to shield her. He loved Tessa so…he bowed his head, right there at the desk he was using.

Dear Lord, I know it's taken me a while. Thank You for finally prying open my eyes and my heart.

"Donnelly, I thought you were out of here," the engineer he'd been working with said. They'd finished the critical jobs, so Josh was free to leave at noon, rather than after work on Friday.

Josh lifted his head. "Cleaning up." He made a show of closing his laptop and putting an extraneous pen in the desk drawer. "It's been great working with you and your team."

"Same here," the engineer said. "Anytime you want to come back, give me a shout."

"I appreciate it." Josh stood, tucked his laptop under his left arm and shook hands with the engineer.

Four hours later, he hopped out of his truck at the Majestic, whistling the Resurrection Light song that had been on the radio. On his way to the apartment, he'd seen his father's truck and figured he and Tessa must still be at the theater, probably celebrating the building inspector's sign-off on the work. He wiped his hands down the sides of his pants and flung open the door, anticipating the look of happy surprise he hoped to see on Tessa's face. What he saw stopped him dead. They were celebrating all right.

Tessa and his father sat across from each other at one of the café tables, his father's back to the door. An open bottle of wine and a glass stood in the center of the table. They each had a hand around the bottle.

Rage consumed Josh. He stormed over and yanked his father's chair around toward him. "How could you? Haven't you ruined enough in my life?" he shouted in his father's face before looking across the table at Tessa. She held fast to the wine bottle, an odd sheen in her eyes. "Didn't I tell you he'd do this?"

Tessa dropped her head, but not her grip, refusing to meet his gaze.

Josh swallowed to stop himself from being sick to his stomach. He'd seen that look before on his father's face.

"Son." His father placed his hand on Josh's forearm.

"Don't *Son* me. You're no father to me, to any of us." Josh grabbed his father's shirtfront and pulled him out of the chair. "Go, get out of here. I don't want you near Tessa or me ever again."

"Stop!" Tessa screamed. "Just stop. It wasn't your father. It was me."

Josh released his father. "What?"

She released the bottle. "I bought the wine after Jerry left. He came back for his watch and found me…"

Josh stared at her in disbelief.

His father's nod confirmed what she'd said.

He closed his eyes, needing to black out the picture of Tessa he was seeing. "You were helping Tessa. Sober support." Josh's voice trailed off. His father… Tessa. A long-blocked-off spot inside him opened. "I'm sorry, Dad. I saw you. I lost my temper."

"I understand," his father said with tears in his eyes.

Josh did, too, seeing his father in the present, not the past. He offered his hand and when his father took it, Josh pulled him into a bear hug. "Thanks."

His father hugged him back. "I owed you."

Josh had a feeling he owed Dad more. "But why?" he asked, looking from his father to Tessa and motioning to the wine bottle. "Didn't the inspector sign off?" He glanced around the room, unable to think of anything else that could have pushed Tessa over the edge.

"No, he did sign off. That was the problem," she said.

Josh's insides churned with confusion. "I don't understand."

His father reached by him and picked up the wine bottle. "I'll put this over here." He placed it on another table. "You can take care of it after you talk. Tessa, we're on for the Saranac meeting tonight?"

"Yes, I need it. You'll pick me up at the house?"

"Sure thing," Jerry said.

Josh smiled at his father and moved the chair he'd been sitting in around next to Tessa. "Tell me about it," he said when he heard the outside door click behind his father.

"The other day when you called and I had to take another call. It was about the stage lights. They were supposed to be delivered to the shipping facility in Ticonderoga but didn't make it."

Josh looked past her to the stage and the lights.

"They were delivered to Saratoga instead. Jerry and I drove down and got them."

Josh drummed his fingers silently on his thigh, wanting to push Tessa to get to the point but sensing she needed to tell things in her own fashion.

"We installed them with Neal's help yesterday, and when we tested them, the circuit breaker blew. Neal installed a new one and it blew, too."

"So you don't have any stage lights?"

"No, we do. It turned out the circuit box amperage was too low. Neal had to put in a new higher amperage box. I used your rent check for it."

"That's good, isn't it?" As with a lot of other things he'd missed, he hadn't realized she was that close on money with the renovations.

"Too good. We kept running up against obstacles and the Lord provided. But when the building inspector gave us the go-ahead for the Monday opening, I should have been psyched. Instead, I felt nothing, less than nothing. Hollow."

Josh placed his right arm on the table and leaned forward. "This was your dream. You've been talking about it almost as long as I've known you."

"It was what I wanted. And when you said you were taking the job in Boston, I told myself if I didn't have you, I *had* to have the theater. I've got the theater, and I feel no sense of accomplishment. Like I said, nothing."

"Whoa, who said I took a job in Boston?"

"You, Monday on the phone."

He took the note of irritation that had seeped into her voice as a positive. It certainly beat the despondency she'd been drowning in.

"You asked me if I could give up the theater and come to Boston with you and hung up before I could answer."

"Wait." He jerked straight. "Back up. What do you mean, if you didn't have me?"

The corners of Tessa's mouth curved up in a weak smile. "Think about it."

He slid his left arm around her shoulder and pulled her to him. "You've had me since the day we met. It took me this long to own up to it."

She leaned her head on his shoulder. "I did tell your father that I thought your skull was made of titanium."

Josh laughed. That was his Tessa. *His* Tessa. He liked the sound of that.

"Let's take care of the wine," she said.

"I'll do it." He jumped to his feet.

"No, I have to."

They walked to the kitchen and Tessa lifted the wine bottle over the sink but didn't pour it down the drain. It hit him like a punch to the solar plexus. *She had no more control over alcohol than his father did.*

"Part of me still doesn't want to do this." The bottle wobbled in her hand.

He unconsciously stepped back, and Tessa tilted her head to look up at him, her gaze clear and direct.

"I know that—now."

She accepted his admission and tipped the bottle over.

He placed his hands on her shoulders, bent down and pressed his lips softly against hers. The sweetness was almost too much to bear. When he lifted his head, she put her arms over his, hands on his shoulders, and studied him.

"I love you, Joshua Donnelly."

Still racing from their kiss, his pulse went into overdrive. "And I love you, Tessa Hamilton."

She rose on her toes, her face lifted to him. "I believe you do."

Those words filled his heart to bursting and then some. He pulled her close and kissed her again with every ounce of love he had for her, accepting her love in return.

Epilogue

~~

Five months later

The unseasonable late fall heat was unbearable, worse than anything Josh had ever experienced, even during his National Guard tour of Afghanistan. A rivulet of sweat ran down his back. He wanted to pull at his collar so he could breathe, cool off his back. But people would see him. He looked at Connor in front of him, ready to officiate, Jared, his best man, beside him and his father beside Jared. To add to the torture, they all grinned at him. He and Tessa should have eloped.

The *Lohengrin* wedding march began and Josh shivered, the heat of a moment ago suddenly gone. Tessa appeared on her father's arm, a vision in a froth of white. He stood mesmerized. Then he saw it, there nestled in the yellow roses in her bouquet where only someone on the raised altar might see it. A fluffy stuffed yellow chick. He choked back a laugh, remembering their dance at Connor's wedding. Best buds is how they'd started and what they'd always be, that and so much more. His vision blurred. Must be dust in his eye. He blinked Tessa back into focus and watched her father lift her veil and kiss her on the cheek before whispering something in her ear. She'd worn her hair down as he liked it. He blinked again. Hadn't Connor had the church cleaned for the ceremony?

Tessa handed her bouquet to her grandmother, who she'd chosen to be her matron of honor, and took her place beside him. His muscles turned to spaghetti. She was so beautiful it hurt. She returned his gaze, admiration and something more shining in her eyes. Then she grinned and he straightened to his full height, offering up a quick prayer in the moment before Connor started the ceremony.

Dear Lord, give me the strength to be all Tessa deserves me to be. Help me to show her the boundless love only You know that I have for her.

"Good morning," Connor said. "Today we're gathered here in the sight of God to celebrate one of life's greatest moments, to give recognition to the worth and beauty of love and to add our best wishes and blessings to the words uniting my brother Joshua Michael Donnelly and Tessa Marie Hamilton in holy matrimony.

"Marriage is a most honorable estate, created and instituted by God, signifying unto us the mystical union, which also rests between Christ and the Church; so, too, may this marriage be adorned by true and abiding love…"

Josh tried to keep his attention on Connor's words, but Tessa's nearness and his joyful wonderment at her becoming his wife kept distracting him.

"Joshua, what token do you give as a pledge of the sincerity of your vows?"

Jared nudged him. "A ring," Josh said.

"Tessa, what token do you give as a pledge of the sincerity of your vows?"

"A ring." She took Josh's ring from her grandmother.

"Please join hands and repeat after me," Connor said.

Following Connor, Josh repeated the words he'd committed to memory. "I, Joshua Michael Donnelly, take you, Tessa Marie Hamilton, to be my wedded wife, to live together in marriage. I promise to love you, comfort you, honor and be with you *for better or worse…*"

Josh didn't care if everyone heard his emphasis on *better or worse*. It was what was in his heart, what Tessa needed from him. And he had no doubts the better would far outweigh the worse.

"For richer or poorer, in sickness and health, and forsaking all others, be faithful only to you, for as long as we both shall live." His hands trembled as he slid the wedding band onto Tessa's finger.

With a shy smile that spoke her joy to him, Tessa did the same, the contrast between the softness of her fingers and steadiness of her hands as she slipped the ring onto his finger nearly brought him to his knees with his love for her.

"Josh and Tessa," Connor said, "insomuch as the two of you have agreed to live together in matrimony, have promised your love for each other by these vows, the giving of these rings and the joining of your hands, I now pronounce you husband and wife. May the Lord bless you and keep you, lift up His countenance unto you and give you peace."

"Congratulations," Connor said then turned to Josh, adding, "Bro," for their ears only. "You may kiss your bride."

Josh sealed his promise to Tessa and she to him. They joined hands and turned to their friends and family.

"And now," Connor said, "I present Joshua and Tessa Donnelly."

Josh squeezed Tessa's hand and she squeezed it back.

He bent to her ear. "So far, this marriage thing is okay," he said.

Their wedding went on record as the only one at Hazardtown Community Church where the ceremony ended with the bride knocking the groom in the shoulder.

* * * * *

Pick up these previous DONNELLY BROTHERS *stories from Jean C. Gordon:*

Hometown boys make good...and find love.

WINNING THE TEACHER'S HEART
HOLIDAY HOMECOMING

You may also enjoy these other books from
Jean C. Gordon set in the town of Paradox Lake

SMALL-TOWN SWEETHEARTS
SMALL-TOWN DAD
SMALL-TOWN MOM
SMALL-TOWN MIDWIFE

All available now from Love Inspired!

Find more great reads at www.LoveInspired.com

Dear Reader,

Thank you for choosing to read *The Bachelor's Sweetheart*. I hope you enjoyed Josh and Tessa's story. Of all the books I've written, this book was the hardest to write and, ultimately, the most rewarding.

I've seen firsthand the toll alcoholism, any addiction, takes on family and friends. Josh and his brothers have dealt with their father's alcoholism most of their lives. Tessa and her family with hers only more recently. Tessa and Josh's story is a tribute to what love can overcome when it has the power of God behind it.

To keep in touch with me, please sign up for my author newsletter at JeanCGordon.com. And feel free to email me at JeanCGordon@gmail.com or snail mail me at PO Box 113, Selkirk, NY 12158. You can also visit me at Facebook.com/JeanCGordon.author or Tweet me at @JeanCGordon.

Blessings,
Jean C. Gordon

COMING NEXT MONTH FROM
Love Inspired®

Available August 23, 2016

HIS AMISH SWEETHEART
Amish Hearts • by Jo Ann Brown

When Esther Stoltzfus's childhood crush, Nathaniel Zook, returns to their Amish community and asks for help with his farm—and an orphaned boy in need—will their friendship blossom into a happily-ever-after?

THE RANCHER'S HOMECOMING
The Prodigal Ranch • by Arlene James

Rex Billings has come home to Straight Arrow Ranch to help his ailing father, and is in desperate need of a housekeeper. With her fine cooking, single mom Callie Deviner seems the perfect candidate—for the job and to be his partner for life.

REUNITING WITH THE COWBOY
Texas Cowboys • by Shannon Taylor Vannatter

Having rodeo cowboy Cody Warren move in next door might just be Ally Curtis's second chance with the boy who got away. But can she trust that the charming bull rider is ready to settle down for good?

FALLING FOR THE SINGLE DAD
by Lisa Carter

Single dad Weston Clark is taken aback when his daughter forms an instant bond with veterinarian Caroline Duer. As they work together to save a wounded sea turtle, can the former coast guard commander make room in his life for a new wife?

THE SOLDIER'S SURPRISE FAMILY
by Jolene Navarro

Former soldier Garrett Kincaid had no plans for a family, until he discovers he has a son he never knew existed. Now his child and the lovely new nanny he's hired are quickly capturing his heart.

HER TEXAS HERO
Texas Sweetheart • by Kat Brookes

Single mom Audra Marshall realizes that her fresh start means accepting Carter Cooper's help in fixing up her new house—so she trades home-cooked meals for labor. But can she exchange the hurts from her past for a new chance at forever?

REQUEST YOUR FREE BOOKS!

2 FREE INSPIRATIONAL NOVELS

PLUS 2
FREE
MYSTERY GIFTS

Love Inspired®

LI15

*When Esther Stoltzfus's childhood crush,
Nathaniel Zook, returns to their Amish community
and asks for help with his farm—and an orphaned
boy in need—will their friendship blossom
into a happily-ever-after?*

*Read on for a sneak preview of
HIS AMISH SWEETHEART by Jo Ann Brown,
available September 2016 from Love Inspired!*

"Are you sure you want Jacob to stay with you?" Esther asked.

"I'm sure staying at my farm is best for him now," Nathaniel said. "The boy needs something to do to get his mind off the situation, and the alpacas can help."

Nathaniel held his hand out to assist Esther onto the seat of the buggy.

She regarded him with surprise, and he had to fight not to smile. Her reaction reminded him of Esther the Pester from their childhood, who'd always asserted she could do anything the older boys did...and all by herself.

Despite that, she accepted his help. The scent of her shampoo lingered in his senses. He was tempted to hold on to her soft fingers, but he released them as soon as she was sitting. He was too aware of the *kinder* and other women gathered behind her.

She picked up the reins and leaned toward him. "If it becomes too difficult for you, bring him to our house."

"We'll be fine." At that moment, he meant it. When her bright blue eyes were close to his, he couldn't imagine being anything but fine.

Then she looked away, and the moment was over. She slapped the reins and drove the wagon toward the road. He watched it go. A sudden shiver ran along him. The breeze was damp and chilly, something he hadn't noticed while gazing into Esther's pretty eyes.

The sound of the rattling wagon vanished in the distance, and he turned to see Jacob standing by the fence, his fingers through the chicken wire again in the hope an alpaca would come to him. The *kind* had no idea of what could lie ahead for him.

Take him into Your hands, Lord. He's going to need Your comfort in the days to come. Make him strong to face what the future brings, but let him be weak enough to accept help from us.

Taking a deep breath, Nathaniel walked toward the boy. He'd agreed to take care of Jacob and offer him a haven at the farm. Now he had to prove he could.

Don't miss
HIS AMISH SWEETHEART by Jo Ann Brown,
available September 2016 wherever
Love Inspired® books and ebooks are sold.

www.LoveInspired.com

Turn your love of reading into rewards you'll love with
Harlequin My Rewards

**Join for FREE today at
www.HarlequinMyRewards.com**

Earn **FREE BOOKS** of your choice.

Experience **EXCLUSIVE OFFERS** and contests.

Enjoy **BOOK RECOMMENDATIONS**
selected just for you.

PLUS! Sign up now
and get **500** points
right away!

Earn
FREE
REWARDS
HarlequinMyRewards.com
Join
Today!

MYR16R